ABOUT THE AUTHOR

Glenda Guest grew up in the wheatbelt of Western Australia, and that land  ing. Since leaving the west, s ltry towns in Victoria, New S ital Territory and south-east nat add to the richness that draw on for their fiction. She is currently living in the Blue Mountains, enjoying being a 'mountain-woman'.

Glenda has had stories and poetry published in various anthologies and journals, and has been invited to contribute to experimental group writing. Chapters from the novel *Siddon Rock* have been published in the journal *Coastlines Cultural Magazine*, which is a joint Australian-Indonesian venture, and the online magazine *Spiny Babbler*. She has had support from artsACT, the arts support organisation of the Australian Capital Territory, for time-out at Varuna, in Katoomba, where the first draft of the novel was written. Glenda works as a freelance writer, reviewer and editor, and teaches occasionally at Macquarie and Griffith Gold Coast universities.

WWW.GLENDAGUEST.COM

SIDDON
ROCK

GLENDA GUEST

SIDDON ROCK

VINTAGE BOOKS
Australia

A Vintage book
Published by Random House Australia Pty Ltd
Level 3, 100 Pacific Highway, North Sydney NSW 2060
www.randomhouse.com.au

First published by Vintage in 2009

Addresses for companies within the Random House Group can be found
at www.randomhouse.com.au/offices

National Library of Australia
Cataloguing-in-Publication Entry

Guest, Glenda.
Siddon rock.

ISBN 978 1 74166 640 3 (pbk).

A823.4

Cover and internal design by Sandy Cull, gogogingko
Typeset in Minion 11.5/15.25 pt by Midland Typesetters, Victoria
Printed and bound by Griffin Press

For my family, Colin, Zoë and Michael,
who thought this was the never-ending story.

ABERLINE FAMILY TREE

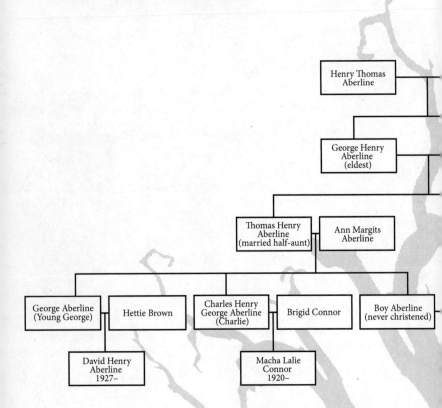

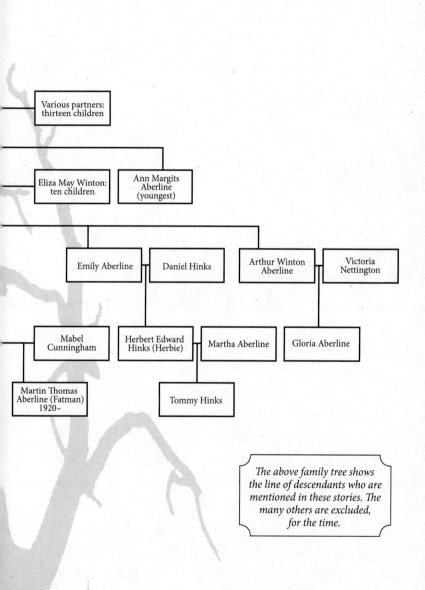

Various partners:
thirteen children

Eliza May Winton:
ten children

Ann Margits
Aberline
(youngest)

Emily Aberline

Daniel Hinks

Arthur Winton
Aberline

Victoria
Nettington

Mabel
Cunningham

Herbert Edward
Hinks (Herbie)

Martha Aberline

Gloria Aberline

Martin Thomas
Aberline (Fatman)
1920–

Tommy Hinks

*The above family tree shows
the line of descendants who are
mentioned in these stories. The
many others are excluded,
for the time.*

PART ONE

CHAPTER ONE

A HOME-COMING DISTURBS THE TOWN

The day of the week that Macha came home became a source of contention, with some saying Saturday and others saying Wednesday. Someone even suggested a Sunday, but everyone knew better than that as there are no trains on a Sunday. What was generally agreed on, however, was that, unlike many who went to that war, Macha Connor came home.

WHEN THE TRAIN REACHED THE TOP OF ITS CLIMB Macha threw the jacket out the window, where it caught in a tree at the side of the track. There it hung like a khaki ghost. At the one and only river crossing the shirt, tie, belt, trousers and underpants landed on the dry river-bed, looking for all the world like abandoned body parts as they spread across the grey sand and rocks.

The train pushed on slowly all that day and into the night, until it arrived at the small tin shed and water tower that was the junction between northern and eastern lines. There the driver uncoupled the engine, which steamed away to the north leaving behind the wheat bins, goods carriages, and the passenger dog-box.

There was no moon this night, and no sound. Not a dingo howl nor a soft cough of kangaroo, and the dry inland night was undisturbed by the wings or cries of night birds. Macha stayed at the window sighting up at the angle of stars she knew as the Southern Cross, trying to match the rifle's cross-hairs with the dead light of five stars as they made a slow and icily glittering cartwheel in the sky.

The return of daylight saw Macha still kneeling at the window watching past the horizon, the rifle loosely cradled in one arm and the other warming across her naked belly. During the night another engine had arrived on the eastern line, and the train bumped and groaned before it settled into a long, slow rock on rails that ran as straight as a die for a hundred miles.

At the beginning of the plains the animals started. A giant red kangaroo lay against the fence beside the track. A little further on there was another, with two emus and a wombat all in a heap, then more, and more. The fence held them back, the piles of dead animals with pelt and flesh diminishing into strips and scraps that would blow across the flat paddocks and roll into fur-balls, to catch on the strand of barbed wire. The telegraph wire, drooped between leaning poles, sagged under the weight of dying birds with glazed yellow eyes, watching the train pass. From the crossbars of the poles, bats with wings folded in penitence hung like black pears rotting from the frost, dropping, as they died, with a dull smack onto the parched ground.

Macha watched the bones appear, protruding from the mass of bodies like white shoots from damp earth. She raised the rifle to a naked shoulder and sighted the familiar cross-hairs at the mass of fur and feathers. *Bang*, she said softly. *Bang*. And so she stayed at the window until the train stopped at the siding before the town of Siddon Rock.

Feeling the steadiness beneath her, Macha stepped down. When the train moved on suddenly, leaving her standing in the powdery dirt, she marched along the centre of the narrow road that ran next to the railway track, towards Siddon Rock.

The town was quiet at this time between close of business and tea-time. There had been a small crowd waiting under the welcoming banner when the train arrived at five o'clock. They were perplexed and a little annoyed to find the small passenger carriage at the rear of the goods van was empty, and now they had gone home or to the pub.

The banner was draped across Wickton Street, the main street of Siddon Rock, anchored between the war memorial and the eaves of the Farmers' Co-op. *Welcome home Mach*, it said, and between *Welcome* and *home* was a likeness of Winston Churchill, recognisable by the large cigar held between vee-d fingers. The painted smile was not quite right, and there was a disturbing suggestion of a sneer in the crescent of red paint. It was this that Macha blew apart as she entered the town.

Ever since that day, people in the town remember that when Macha came home she walked into town as naked as the day she was born, except for well-worn and shining boots, a dusty slouch hat, and the .303 rifle she held across her waist.

It was the shot, they said, that disturbed the rock and set off strange vibrations. The bullet tore through Churchill's face, hit the silo at the far end of Wickton Street, ricocheted off the rock from which the town took its name, and in its dying fall struck a glancing blow at the three-faced clock in the war memorial obelisk. The story goes that the hands of the clock-face in the centre spun madly and finally came to rest together, holding each other up, so to speak, pointing to the number twelve – even though the other two clock-faces showed it was just after six-thirty.

The sound of the shot shattered the dense inland twilight, that time when the world is muffled between the clarity of day and the dark softness of night. The white cockatoos that had settled in the pepper trees of the station-yard erupted upwards with banshee screeches, throwing themselves indignantly around the war memorial and tangling in the damaged banner. Up they swarmed above the town, a squarking, squalling gang bullying its way through the fluttery brown wrens, willy wagtails and sparrows. Up they soared, up and up again, a fractured, clamouring ghost spiralling into the greying sky above the town.

It's God's-eye view here. A little further up, another circle of the spiral, the edge of the world will appear. But here is enough; no need for more. Look one way and see the darkening heart of the inland; look the other way and there is the pink reflection of the setting sun on the horizon. Below is the brown land, the skin of the earth. Near the town, paddocks make a subdued mosaic: the ochre of neatly ploughed furrows contrasts with the pale stubble of last year's harvest. Dark patches of uncleared bush appear too raw and threatening against the neatness of the farmlands. The salt lakes spreading across the southern ends of the farms of Young George Aberline and Brigid Connor glitter pinkly in the last rays of the sun.

Directly below is a pile of rocks that from here looks like a handful of dropped stones. The locals call this pile the rock. At the border of the town and the rock a tall wheat silo stands, a stone finger to the sky. The small grid of streets that form the township of Siddon Rock runs into the tracks winding through and around the rock, tying each to the other in a mobile sort of way. The railway track is a stitching of neat needle-marks across the land, coming from where you cannot see, and disappearing into the dark of encroaching night.

It's quiet now. The cockatoos have formed into a silent wheeling pattern, waiting to return to their pepper trees.

In a few moments Abe Simmons will start the town electricity generator, and the hospital and the pub will light up like twin beacons. Marge Redall jokes regularly that the town will always be here, clustered around those two places. People need the hospital to heal broken bodies, she says, and the pub to tend to broken minds. But where the hotel kitchen is bustling in preparation for evening meals, the kitchen of the hospital will stay dark, as Old Nell has well and truly finished for the day – she's dried the tea-time dishes, hung the tea-towel on the rail in front of the fireplace and walked out the door. Now she's heading to the path that will take her home over the rock.

At the pub Marge, Bluey Redall and Kelpie Crush work the bar for the larger than normal crowd of drinkers. Kelpie moves quickly and quietly among the tables collecting glasses, emptying ashtrays, generally rounding up the rubbish. The bar is dusky with smoke, from cigarettes and from the fire that Peter Mather has put a match to. He's possessive of the fire, is Peter. Bluey Redall allows Peter to think of it as his, as he does of the chair next to it where he sits every night, summer or winter.

The town settles, turning on lights and pulling curtains, putting up the barricades against the encroaching night. At 16 Whistler's Way, Gloria Aberline lights the ready-set fire in the lounge-room grate. The kerosene-soaked lighters catch easily and the reflected flames dance a bizarre rhythm on unshaded window-glass. Next door her friend and only confidante, Martha Hinks, pours herself a sherry – sweet – and opens the local newspaper at the kitchen table. In the house by the railway station Mister Placer, who likes his evening meal early, shakes out a table napkin and waits for his wife Mary to bring the plates. Siggy Butow, in the manse opposite the Methodist church, is checking the boxes delivered from the Farmers' Co-op that morning, rummaging – that's the word Siggy uses, 'rummaging' – around for ingredients to make a meal. He'd have more choice, if he shopped for himself.

Doctor Allen opens the door of the surgery attached to his home near the hospital. He ushers out Mrs Abe Simmons and the door shuts behind them with a tired sigh.

Doctor Allen holds her arm as they walk the few steps to the street. *The baby's doing well, you know*, he says. *Just make sure you rest with your legs up during the day.* Mrs Simmons turns towards the power station, and Doctor Allen heads to the comfort of the pub and two fingers of scotch whisky. He never takes any more, in case he's needed during the night. As he passes the school he calls to Harry Best, who bookmarks where he's at in Ovid's *Metamorphoses*, and joins his friend. Harry is in no rush to go home; he always looks forward to their conversations.

In the last house on the last street before the town turns to farmland Maureen Mather struggles to get off her bed. The cockatoos' shrieks disturbed her from her aspirin-induced doze, and she has woken sweating and trembling. *I'm coming*, she calls thickly. *I'm coming. Just gotta get awake first.* She is still in her nightmare of broken bodies and minds in a makeshift tent-hospital, and her patients need her; but her legs are not cooperating as she reaches for the wheelchair at the side of her bed.

Way over, hidden from the town by the bulk of the rock, Sybil Barber's house at the edge of the lake is dark. Sybil is still at Barber's Butchery & Bakery scrubbing the blocks and counter ready for the next day. Sybil's shop is the only one showing light as Albey Carey the pharmacist and the Farmers' Co-op both close at five-thirty sharp. At Meakins' Haberdashery and Ladies & Men's Apparel, Alistair Meakins stands in the recess of the entrance where his black suit – which, the town ladies whisper, makes him look like an undertaker – blends with the shadows.

11

In the darkening silence the cockatoos drop back to their roost in the pepper trees in the station-yard, and the town appears to settle into its normal night.

Alistair was a mathematical type of person: he liked rows of figures and neatly tidied shelves; his daily records of sales were immaculate and his ledger was a wonder of precision. Ladies' shoes were always easily to hand, arranged strictly in their code numbers and half sizes with the front of the boxes just touching the shelf edge. The messy items of haberdashery, such as lace and elastic, buttons and hooks-and-eyes, were stored in shelves of glass-fronted drawers so they were neat and tidy, but also easily seen by Alistair's customers.

Alistair saw the world as intersecting lines and spaces. His window display often had a background of ribbon lattice in suitable colours, usually bright yellows and greens for spring, russets and gold for autumn displays and cool blues for winter. He rarely used summer colours, saying to his customers, *Summer is a blast from hell without red blaring into the street, to make us feel worse.*

As Macha marched into town with the rifle held stiffly in front of her he saw angles: broad shoulders that tapered to the waist, and straight long lines of her legs; small triangles of breasts barely changed the sweep of chest, and sharp elbows rested at her waist. Pale patches of freckles emphasised the planes of her cheekbones and made them look high and dangerous. In the half-light of dusk Macha's nakedness glowed like white camellias, but her still features were hidden by the slouch hat.

Alistair looked along the street to see who else was watching. He went into the shop and locked the door behind him. He walked past the orderly rows of sewing goods and skeins of wool that hung on long hooks on the wall, past the store dummies displaying cotton frocks, and into a curtained alcove.

In the fitting room Alistair stood looking at the poster of a woman draped elegantly against a railing. Behind her the Eiffel Tower appeared to lean towards her, in wonder at her beauty. But it was the image of the dress that Alistair caressed, running his hand down the flowing skirt. No ordinary dress this one, it fell in long folds from a tightly belted bodice into a skirt that swirled around slender legs encased in fine nylons. *Grey*, Alistair thought, *definitely silver-grey silk faille. And that little white Peter Pan collar. The hat, black with a black net veil. Just perfect.* Alistair put his hand over the one word on the poster – Dior – pressing the palm down firmly as if to draw an essence from the curving letters. To Alistair's admiring eye the model's delicate features looked amazingly like those of Macha Connor.

Alistair turned from the French perfection and looked into the mirror. His plump softness overflowed the glass and made him sigh. From the region of his heart came a green glow that made him look taller, straighter and more angular, and his reddish complexion faded to white petals touched with brown freckles of frost. Alistair put on a broad-brimmed hat, pulling it down so that his light brown eyes became deep and mysterious. With one hand he pulled his full-cut white shirt firmly so that his breasts flattened into tipped diamonds which he brushed lightly with the back of his other hand. Alistair held the pose until the green glow faded. He placed the hat back on the shelf, left the shop by the door that opened into the back lane and walked through the dust and dry grass to his house.

That night, when Alistair completed his ledger entries for the day, he wrote neatly at the bottom of the credit column: *Macha Connor came home*. And at the corresponding debit column: *This is unbalanced*.

Sybil Barber was an observer, aware of the nuances of human foibles. She watched the daily interactions of the town through screens of fine mesh netting that kept flies from trays of soft dark kidneys and livers and the hanging strips of pale, rough-sided tripe in the display window.

In the waning light Sybil watched Macha, and watched Alistair watching Macha. Further down the street a shaft of light spilled out as Kelpie Crush held open the door of the bar for Gawain Evans. Sybil saw Kelpie pick up beer glasses left on the window-ledges of the pub and stack them in a precarious pile up his arm. He paused as Macha marched past.

Of the many things that Sybil Barber knew about the town of Siddon Rock, one was that Kelpie Crush would not eat the plain, robust meals prepared by Marge Redall at the

Railway and Traveller's Hotel where he was the barman. He, Kelpie, was a tender and gentle cook who subscribed to a French trade magazine for chefs, and he preferred the delicate flesh of veal and lamb – when it was available – to the stronger meat of beef or mutton. *There's something about the meat here that's different,* he said to Sybil when he first arrived in town. *A sort of underlying tang that's not there in city meat. And it's a bit tougher.*

It's the feed, Sybil said, *the saltbush. And everything here grows tougher than in the city. It has to, to survive.*

Each week Sybil chose her beasts from the local herds and flocks, feeling along rib-cages for firmness without too much fat. Not that this country encouraged fat. The beasts produced here by the dry forage of stubble and saltbush were solid and sturdy animals, and Sybil knew well the shape of flesh and muscle concealed by a fine layer of tissue that tied skin to carcass. *No-one in the town,* she thought, *no-one except myself knows what to expect when that smooth cover is broken.* She was deft and quick in separating the skin from the carcass and quite liked the silky smoothness of the meat as she jointed and boned the various cuts. It was, she thought, similar to the feel of the thighs of her men as they lay along her, although not as warm.

Sybil watched Gawain Evans pause and glance towards her shop, then turn and walk towards his home. She knew, though, that when he strolled up the street each day from the Council Offices where he worked, his real, hidden desire was not the currant bun he asked her for. She had experienced the surprising strength of this mild-looking man with the dark, slicked-down hair, and was happy to take him into her bed occasionally, but not into her life.

As she watched Alistair Meakins watching Macha, Sybil knew that for his meal tonight he would have two lamb cutlets, mashed potato and tinned peas. She wondered, not for the first time, why he had not visited her at night. She had suggested it once, but he had doffed his hat to her and said formally, *My dear, thank you for the offer. You can be sure that, if I ever feel the urge for female companionship, it will be yourself I will seek.*

At the time Sybil had wondered why someone as obviously sophisticated as Alistair would come to a place like Siddon Rock, but pushed the thought aside.

As for Macha Connor, Sybil Barber considered that she didn't carry enough flesh to feed a crow, let alone a hungry man.

Sybil set the starter for the next morning's bread batch – ten wholemeal, fifteen white and five jubilee twist covered the regulars and a few spare – checked that the floors and pine chopping block were spotless, and then let herself out into the chill, still evening.

Kelpie Crush stood with glasses stacked up his arm, propping open the swinging door to the street with a polished boot. He saw Alistair standing in the shadows of the entrance to Meakins' Haberdashery and Ladies & Men's Apparel. He saw the lights go off in Barber's Butchery & Bakery and knew that Sybil Barber would be watching Macha.

The patrons of the pub saw Kelpie Crush as a quiet, efficient barman who knew everyone's drink and when they were ready for another. He slowed the rate of drinks to some as the evening went on, but did this so that it was not noticed. He heard stories and whispers across the dark wood of the public bar with its brass foot-rail on which farmers, townsmen and the occasional travelling salesman rested their dusty boots or glossy shoes. No-one knew he heard them and no-one heard them from him. The few women who sometimes sat in the Ladies' Lounge found him courteous, but there was no flirtatious tension which was so often found in the slight risqué-ness of the place. It could be said that Kelpie Crush was the perfect barman.

Because of his expertise at the pub some people found it curious when Kelpie pinned a notice on the town noticeboard at the Council Offices, asking if anyone was interested in forming the Siddon Rock Cub Scouts Pack. *What's a barman doing with kids?* they said. Someone, possibly Doctor Allen, spoke with the headmaster, Harry Best, who then had a quiet word with Kelpie one afternoon over a beer.

Harry reported back that he was pleased to say that Kelpie Crush appeared to have excellent credentials, having run such a pack in the city. He was, Harry said, a quiet man who some time before had a nervous breakdown from a high-pressure position in the capital. He had moved to Siddon Rock to avoid the stresses of city living and to indulge himself in his hobby of collecting moths and bush insects. He took the bar job because it was available when he arrived in town. As everyone knew that paying work was difficult to come by for someone not able to cope with the rigours of farm labouring, the discussion of suitability was dropped.

When Kelpie's passion for moths and insects became known, a town project was gradually formed as people brought any unusual-looking bugs to the hotel. But there were no invitations to view the collection, although Kelpie had been heard to say that he would, one day when it was complete, show the work in the foyer of the Council Offices.

Now, as Macha marched down the street, Kelpie watched through the partly closed door. He admired Macha's thin, boyish shape for a moment and then turned back to the unusually large crowd of drinkers at the bar.

To reach her home from the town Nell followed a path that started at the tall, round wheat silo built into the base of the rock at the edge of the town. This path wound to the top of the rock, negotiating small canyons and gullies. It wandered past an occasional quandong tree or small patch of sandy soil where, in spring, pink and white everlasting flowers grew fragilely against the dark walls of the rock.

The wheat silo dominated the town. No low metal and timber container this, it was built soon after the first wheat crop was harvested in the district. Modelled on the French lighthouses of the Atlantic Ocean, it stood tall and proud against the sea of bushland that surrounded the settlement. A veritable light in the wilderness, the early farmers and settlers declared. A silo to be proud of, to fill with golden grain for the European markets. The architect and builder – whose name had long since been erased from the dedication plaque by the sand-blast of summer dust storms – found the perfect site on the base of the rock. A good level area for the road and railway and plenty of loose stone for the walls of the silo was what he had looked for, and found. He drilled foundations into the rock itself and bound the building to it. He graded and smoothed a circular road for easy access. He designed and patented an unloading system that carried the grain to the top of the building from the carts and trucks that waited in line, and then poured it through a hatch into the vast belly of the silo. *This will be here a thousand years from now*, he said, and so still say the people of Siddon Rock, to this day.

On the day Macha Connor returned from war, Nell was on her way home from the hospital when she heard the rifle crack. Impelled by an inherited memory of death by gunfire, she dropped to the ground, falling just as the bullet from Macha's rifle hit the silo tower where she usually leaned to take off her shoes. The abrasion it left in the stonework shone like fool's gold as the bullet ricocheted towards the town clock. There it bounced off the central clock face and dropped to the top of three wide steps that led to the lists of names engraved on the obelisk.

Nell climbed higher up the path and turned to look down the main street. There she saw Macha marching towards her home at the Two Mile. Back along the railway line, in the setting sun she saw the dead fruit bats crisping in the coming frost and, much further back, dingoes shying away from the discarded uniform jacket hanging ghostlike in a tree. She looked at the pale figure in the street and understood that most of Macha had come home.

᠕

When Macha marched into Siddon Rock she followed the narrow, gravelled road which gained shops on one side and the railway yard and station building on the other. This was Wickton Street. It continued past the Council Offices and hall, the silo, and a few sunburnt houses clinging to the skirts of the town; there Wickton Street once again became a country road as it curved around the rock and away towards the interior.

At the intersection of this road and the Two Mile Lakes Road, Fatman Aberline caught up with Macha, the growl of his motorbike loud in the silence of the surrounding bush. *C'mon, Mach*, he said. *C'mon. Get on the back and I'll take you home. C'mon, Mach. Let me help.* Macha tramped on.

Brigid Connor's old Dodge truck laboured towards them with farm dogs hanging off the back, and stopped in front of Macha. Leaving Granna in the cab with her foot on the brake, Brigid strode towards her daughter with her arms wide for an embrace, but Macha appeared not to see her and continued her march, the rifle still held across her waist.

Brigid ran back to the truck and drove it around in a noisy half-circle. Now its lights combined with that of the motorbike and made a clear path down the road, but

Macha marched in the loose gravel at the verge. And so they continued, with Brigid driving the labouring truck behind her daughter, and Fatman Aberline riding at Macha's side, and then ahead in frustration before returning to try again. *C'mon, Mach. I'll take you home. I'm sorry I laughed. Let me help.*

Granna leaned from the cab of the truck and shouted at Fatman, *You. Young Aberline. Leave her alone and go on home. She don't want you around right now.* She slapped Brigid on the arm, *Stop the truck. Let me down. She's left something behind at wherever she's been. She don't need no-one yapping at her.* And Granna walked in the gravel, interposed between Macha and the motorbike until Fatman Aberline gave up and turned back towards the town.

I'll go then, Brigid called over the yelping of the dogs. *I'll see you back at the house,* and the truck rattled off, leaving just the scrunch of gravel under Macha's boots and the smell of petrol floating in the startling silence.

Granna and Macha walked on. Macha staggered occasionally, as if her invisible load was too much to bear. Granna took her arm in support, and then realised that they had been joined by a third person, who was humming gently as she walked, supporting Macha on the other side. She nodded to Nell. *Singing in the dark keeps away the devils,* she said.

This 'un has hers inside, Nell said, and her humming became louder and more rhythmic. Granna started to sing old and familiar words. *Hush little baby don't you cry,* she sang, *you look much better when your eyes are dry.* Nell's

21

pitch changed slightly and added a deeper tone. *And if that horse and cart falls down, you'll still be the sweetest little baby in town.*

Granna found herself walking differently. Her body relaxed and her shoulders dropped and moved in a different rhythm. Her legs seemed to be longer and somehow more flexible as they stretched into deeper strides. She realised then that they were above the gravel road, lifted by their singing.

The voices of the women rose and united as they turned into the home track holding the still-marching Macha between them. In the distance behind them a light shone from the windows of Sybil Barber's house and reflected in the thick waters of the salt lake. Around them dust, dry bush smells and the sharp tang of newly ploughed paddocks blended to a pungent mix. Down the track they glided, over the sheep-grid at the house-paddock and across the hard dirt yard, still supporting Macha above the ground; then onto the wide verandah where the clamouring dogs went silent when they saw them.

Through the back door into the kitchen they went, and down the hall to Macha's room, as Brigid ran ahead to open the door. Nell and Granna stopped singing and lowered Macha to the floor where she marched on the spot. *You can stop marching now*, Granna said. At first Macha seemed not to have heard, but gradually her tempo slowed, and stopped, and she stood there clutching the rifle. The women stood close to steady her if she staggered; but Macha moved the rifle to her shoulder, stepped over the threshold, and the door swung shut behind her.

From that day on Granna saw Nell around the town, and she always waved in recognition and acknowledgement.

CHAPTER TWO

NAMES ARE A SOMETIMES THING

Naming is an important thing, but it's generally done by accident.

HENRY ABERLINE, in the library of Greater Wickton to escape the weather and the appalling splashing from carriage wheels in puddles, read by chance an essay on the *Papilio venenatus Nemo (Mariposidae)*, the elusive poisonous butterfly. The writer of the essay was surprised, nay, astounded, at reports filtering in to the Royal Lepidopterology Society of Great Britain that this rare creature had been sighted by an explorer of the inland plains of Australia. The writer was sceptical as he knew *Papilio venenatus Nemo (Mariposidae)*, although it had not been seen for many years, only inhabited the cooler regions of England, preferring a mild to warm summer for breeding. He was, however, prepared to countenance the supposition that a species of mimetic butterfly had taken on the colouration and habits of *Papilio venenatus* and this was what had been seen.

Henry Aberline had held to the light the fine painting of the butterfly that accompanied the essay, noting that the colours of the wings were etched with black, rather like an overlay. If the picture was held one way the wings looked a dusty and deep red; one could almost call it maroon except for the brightness of the highlights. But looking at it from another angle it could be said that the butterfly was black. He wondered if the butterfly was so coloured or if the artist had a particular talent he wished to display.

Henry looked out the library window, the painting still in his hands. Past the sleet and snow there shone a clear blue and yellow light that showed a broad plain with stands of tall timber. The skies glowed like sapphire and were filled with the jewelled colours of unknown birds and insects. Henry stepped through the window-glass of the library onto the plain, and walked towards a group of exotic-looking people who, he saw, were dark and straight, as if they grew from the land itself. Tall grasses covering the plain swayed in a light breeze and parted before strange animals which were unperturbed by the nearness of the people, who smiled at them as they grazed. Around the animals fluttered hordes of glowing butterflies. One man waved him forward and the rest of the people gathered around as well, welcoming him and offering food and drink. As the group ate, the butterflies alighted on their arms and head with *Papilio venenatus*, a jewel of infinite worth, in the hair of the leading savage, the one with the biggest smile. This man put his arm around Henry's shoulder in a gesture of brotherhood and slowly turned him around so that the whole land appeared to open out before him. He spread his arms. *This is yours*, Henry read of the gesture, *all this beauty is for you*.

Back in the library, Henry Aberline went to the large globe of the world that was fixed in a wooden frame. He found that to see the shape of Australia in its correct position in relation to Europe, he had to twist himself downwards into awkward positions, as a wide wooden ledge hid those countries below the equator. Ignoring the damage to his trousers and the amused glances of people nearby, he lay on the floor and found the area where the butterfly had been reported as seen. *Terra de Leeuwin* was written in the flowing script of the seventeenth century, and under the writing was painted a palm tree with a fabulous winged beast resting on the fronds. When he touched the map a faint vibration tingled up his finger and he could hear a rhythmical thrumming sound that was quite musical. The other side of the mirror, Henry thought – he was quite poetical in his own way – the Antipodes.

That very afternoon Henry Aberline contacted the master at the Liverpool Docks and found that the brigantine *Caroline* was departing the next week. Immediately, he arranged passage to the nearest port in Australia for himself, his boxes of collecting and preserving equipment, various books on lepidopterology and the trunks of clothing selected by a Bond Street outfitter competent in advising the gentleman explorer. He paid fleeting visits to various friends, kissed his parents and bade a glad farewell to middle England.

The journey to Australia was long but uneventful, and when the *Caroline* arrived at the destination and docked at a makeshift jetty, Henry walked the beach and revelled in the sand under his feet, firm in comparison to the ever-shifting ship's deck of the past three months. He could feel his uneasy stomach settling and wondered about the quality, and indeed the quantity, of food in this barren-looking place.

Henry scanned the beach for the figure he remembered so well from his vision. There were many dark figures watching the ship, but Henry could not make out one from another although he was sure his friend would be there to greet him. He approached a group and, in a loud voice so they could understand, tried to describe the person he expected, but eventually realised that any of the group could fit the description. One man stepped forward and said he would take Henry wherever he wanted to go. And so it was agreed.

Henry's guide, whom he called Jack, asked him where he wanted to go. Henry riffled through the smallest of his travelling trunks until he found a picture, which he passed to Jack. *Just find me this butterfly*, he said.

The others of the group gathered around Jack and looked at the small painting with great interest, rubbing their hands across the surface and seeming to comment on the texture of the paper. Henry wondered if they realised this was just a picture of his dream, a representation of what he was looking for. Maybe they thought he wanted Jack to find another painting like the one they examined so closely.

But before Henry could say anything further, Jack waved the picture in the air. *Can find*, he said. *But a lotta walkin'.*

Jack led the party south along the coast then veered away from the coastal dunes into low scrubby bush. Jack and his party slipped easily through the trees, *like they don't even see them*, Henry thought resentfully as he fought his way after his guide. It seemed to him that the trees themselves were against him, edging together into an impermeable thicket, trying to block his way after Jack had passed through.

Each night, as soon as dark fell, Henry entered his tent, wrapped himself in his blanket and slept, exhausted by his battle with the landscape.

Eventually the shape and composition of the scrub changed. Ferns appeared on the forest floor and trees towered above dense undergrowth. *This must have been how Gulliver felt in Brobdingnag*, Henry said to Jack as they gazed upwards to where the top of one forest giant disappeared above all the others.

This Gulliver, Jack said, *he a friend of yours?*

Not exactly, Henry replied. *He's in a story. Not real.*

Jack looked concerned, and laid a friendly hand on Henry's arm. *Pity that*, he said, *that's a real shame.* He paused and looked up at the tall trees, then to where his family had disappeared into the forest. *Our stories now, they real.*

The party travelled further inland and then turned north where the forests thinned to sparsely treed open bushland with altogether different trees. Some were tall with no branches growing from an ethereal white trunk until the high crown burst into the air like a giant flower-head. Some were many-stemmed from the same root, and blood-red. Henry wrote in his journal: *We go ever north. Red is the dominant colour in this place. A perversion of colour, one should say. No green in this hot land, just red soil, high red rocks. Even the trunks of the trees are a reddish colour, as if they do not want to distinguish themselves from their surroundings. And what to make of trees that drop their bark but keep their leaves. Those leaves give little shade and no relief for the unfortunates who stand beneath them, for they turn sideways to the sun, as if the searing rays are too much to bear.*

And the heat was indeed too much to bear for Henry, as they pushed further north and east. But, although his English clothes felt like the heaviest of heavy blankets wrapped around him in the stifling heat of the inland summer, he refused to abandon the high collar and tie or the coat over long trousers. *One must maintain standards,* he wrote. *My father taught me well and I will not go native.*

Jack's people tried to teach Henry how to read the land; how to recognise plants that were edible and tell them apart from those that were not; how to find water; how to judge direction by the way huge termite mounds were sited, miraculously pointing north and south. But in truth it was an impossible task, for Henry could only see the grotesque threat of the bush, and the strangeness of the vast open spaces so filled with difference from the green and cluttered landscape of England. *Even the moors,* he thought, one particularly hot and miserable day, *even the Yorkshire moors are busy and filled with life in comparison to this place.*

He shuddered away when offered food from the campfire, preferring the ever-diminishing rations of hard-tack to the fresh meatiness of a goanna roasted in the ashes of the campfire. Eventually he came to accept fruit and roots, but this was not until close to the end of the journey when his own dry rations were exhausted.

They continued to trek across the country, from east to west and back again, from south to north and then returning, as they followed the flight of the elusive poisonous butterfly. *How do I know* venenatus *is actually here?* Henry said to Jack. *How do I know you aren't just taking my money?*

Look, Jack said, *you can see.* Henry could see nothing on the leaf Jack held for him; it appeared to be just a leaf with the usual vein markings and a brown dot or two. But being of a generally trusting and somewhat slothful nature he continued to follow Jack with no more question as to his honesty.

The party travelled on and on, accompanied by heat, dust and swarms of particularly annoying black flies that crawled into Henry's nose and eyes. They arrived at a place where Jack said they should stop and rest for some days. Henry looked around him. Red dust rose in small eddies from land that was flat and dry, even though he reckoned it was now near the end of winter. It was hard for Henry to tell what season it was, even though they had, by his own calculations, been tracking the *venenatus* butterfly for three hundred and thirty days. Time in this place was a shifting thing, he found, and days slid together with an ease that astounded him, accustomed as he was to the regulated time of middle England. And, if the truth be known, he was tired of this flat country with its endlessness. He was wearying of all this tracking around, and was wondering if it was all for nothing; a chimera. So Henry demurred about staying here, seeing nothing that appealed to him. Jack, however, would not budge. *My mob want to stay here a bit*, he said. *We stay.*

Henry roused the next morning from a broken and troubled sleep. Threads of dreams had led him into cellars and attics where boxes of books formed walls in front of him. Piles of clothing gathered around him, pushing their velvets and laces against him in sensual abandon; old journals and diaries opened themselves and the words of his forebears flew off the pages into the air, clinging to him like the clouds of flies he loathed so much, before fading, leaving just blank pages that dried and blew away.

He stirred from this dark enthralment longing for the sound of wagon wheels over cobblestones, of English voices in conversation. Oh, for the hustle of the markets and the rough cries of the vendors! Ah, the coldly refreshing winters and the soft drift of snow! There was a sentimental remembrance of the murmuring hush of the library at Greater Wickton, and the scholarly discussions in the comfort of an easy chair by the fire. And in the evening, the smell of roasting chestnuts in the snowy streets as he relaxed in a comfortable carriage on the way home, where there awaited friends with whom to enjoy a fine roast beef dinner, a good claret in rare crystal, and a Cuban cigar. What madness had driven him from this elegant life! What bedevilment enticed him to this place that now appeared so like the depictions of hell he had seen in paintings in the Tate Gallery?

At the marginal moment between sleep and wake, Henry decided to end the search and board the first ship home to England. He would take no more discussion about this matter. They would leave this minute. Return to the jetty on the beach and hence back home, away forever from this godforsaken place.

Henry left his tent determined that Jack's mob would pack up immediately, but the sight before him banished any thoughts except those of awe. A floral carpet had bloomed overnight and covered the plains, changing the barren landscape to a multi-hued wonder. An astonishment of blossoms, the like of which he had never known, stretched as far as he could see, to the horizon and beyond, he thought. Maybe it covered the whole vast country from shore to shore.

Henry walked into the exotic garden and plucked handfuls of papery flowers, their unexpected stiffness rustling together like a distant wind. *Weeds among weeds, or flowers with flowers gather'd*, he murmured to himself as he pulled, many plants coming out by the roots. Then he recalled the lines that followed. *No, it was builded far from accident*, he recited as he stood there with his arms full of the flowers called everlastings. *It suffers not in smiling pomp, nor falls / Under the blow of thralled discontent.* He stopped in amazement; that such a message could be sent to him in this place so far from anything he considered civilised. That the desert could bloom into such beauty, and that this spectacle recalled Shakespeare's words to him, must surely be an omen. He was not to turn back, it seemed. He must go on. The butterfly would indeed be his.

Pretty, eh? said Jack. *Anything like this in your England?*

Like this? Henry replied. *No, not like this. Definitely not like this.*

On the seven hundred and sixtieth day the party made its way through thick gimlet scrub and sheltered from the afternoon heat at the base of a low-lying mass of rocks. A woman of Jack's family asked Henry about the butterfly he sought, and what he would do when he found it. *Take it home to England*, Henry said, *to prove that it is here.*

That night as he lay in his blankets under a small tree part-way up the largest rock Henry felt the same dull thrumming rhythm he had heard in the library in the Midlands. He threw off his blankets and rose above the rock, and as he flew over the members of Jack's family sleeping below, through his butterfly eyes he saw them as fragments, and fragments of fragments, and in the fragmentation were the trees and the rock. He tried to look at his wings, to identify himself, but could not see them in the blur of movement that kept him aloft. He flew over the rock, and saw, over the place where he had been sleeping, a hovering cloud of *Papilio venenatus*. He had a surge of sadness of such painful intensity that he cried out in sorrow and dropped down into them where they became as one, and the trembling of their wings beat time with the thrumming of the rock. Henry had become as one with the rock.

When Henry woke the sadness was with him. What had happened to little Hal Aberline, heir apparent to the family cotton mill in Lancashire? Look, there he was as a toddler, riding his wooden horse up and down the driveway of the family home. He loved the cool gardens even then, and liked to go to the stream with Nurse. And later, as a young gentleman, he was on his way to boarding school in Surrey. How sad he looked as he waved goodbye. Such a home-body he was, young Hal, never happier than when riding with Father before breakfast, or taking tea with Mother in the afternoon. What then had driven him to this arid and isolated place – a whim that turned cruel; a fantasy he became enmeshed in, and now could not escape.

So there he sat, under his tree, and would not be moved. He broke a limb from the tree and watched the trunk ooze slow, thick blood until it congealed and scabbed to hide the wound. He watched in dull abstraction the swarms of brown moths that hid from the heat in dark gullies, thinking that their short life would be far preferable to the one he now inhabited.

Henry's male descendants, for at least five generations, would carry the sadness of the Aberlines, and often, like Henry did, find life too much to bear.

Henry stayed under his tree, in bad weather retreating to a small cave. Over the years stories about the Englishman who lived under a tree that grew out of a rock seeped back to the capital, attracting adventurous sightseers to visit the place. Women in particular were drawn to the idea of the romantic adventurer alone in the wilderness. These people would ask Henry why he did not move, at which Henry opened his arms wide, indicating the dull waves of gimlet and mallee scrub that surged from the base of the rock to the horizon. *I will disappear*, he'd say. *It will drown me.*

This answer often did not satisfy those more determined to have a rational explanation, and they'd find members of Jack's family and ask them what had happened. *He's a butterfly*, one said. *He flew*, said another.

What rubbish, the sightseers said, or *absolute balderdash*, and off they'd go to Jack himself and ask him what had happened. *What made Henry Aberline stay at the rock?*

He got tired, Jack always said. *He gotta sit down.*

This seemed entirely logical, and gradually the curves of dark granite that rose above the bush became known as Sitdown Rock.

Occasionally one of the sightseers asked Jack's people if there was another name for the rock. *Yeah*, they'd say, *this Yad Yaddin*. And if there was pressure to give a meaning there would be a shrug and a mumbled reply that sounded like *stay here*. But the listener could not always be sure.

New Wickton, written very small in cursive script on approved maps, was the designated name of the town: an official recognition of the origins of Henry Aberline. But those who first came to the place referred to it as Sitdown Rock, and by popular usage and lazy tongues this became Siddon Rock – and so it remained until there was no other name in the memory of the town.

Macha Connor's great-grandfather was George Henry Aberline, one of the several sons of Henry (for women found the tree on the rock a most romantic place). George Henry proposed marriage to Eliza May Winton, youngest progeny of the Wintons, who were newly arrived from Cheshire.

Eliza May looked at the barren settlement where George suggested they live. She viewed with distaste the shabby tents and lean-to shanties that made up most of the town and which seemed to have no order, apart from two shops that huddled for security close to the pub. She thought of her grandmother's home in Manchester, of how peaceful and calm it was, and considered that she, Eliza May, was entitled to at least this.

Eliza May accepted the proposal of marriage from George Henry. However, she had heard enough stories about Henry Aberline to consider that his disposition towards melancholy and inaction may well have been passed to his son, and so she added the condition that a house must be ready to move into before the marriage could take place. This house was not to be in the town. George was to take up land and they would make their own farm.

With the realisation that a bedroom was necessary for wedded bliss, George considered his options. The few houses in the settlement of Siddon Rock that were neither shanties nor tents were built of lightweight and easily transported tin pressed with stylised swirls of *fleur-de-lys* or other popular European patterns. But it took many months to write an order, mail it to England for the tin sheets to be manufactured and shipped to the port, then carted to Siddon Rock. Neither was he prepared to wait the uncertain length of time for native timber to be ordered, cut, milled, seasoned and transported from the distant forests. As for a brick house, the impossibility of this was overwhelming, what with the cost of transport from elsewhere. Brickworks near the capital were but an idea in the minds of business-men, as a suitable deposit of clay was still being sought.

In short, George decided to buy a house already built, and he set out on his quest.

People in the district soon became accustomed to the ornately twisted and curled chords of music that billowed behind George in red arabesques as he rode through the landscape in search of a house. Although he was no musician, George recognised snatches of Mendelssohn's *Wedding March* that sang out each time he approached a house that was, possibly, for sale. And each time he left unrequited, the chords lost colour and drooped down his back, wilting and straightening like the unravelling ringlets of pale honey-coloured hair tied in bunches each side of Eliza's round, strong face. As the search widened into the surrounding districts, *basso profundo* notes of the nuptial benediction joined the chorus in an increasingly desperate counterpoint. The sound was remarkably similar to the exhortations of Mister Bloom, the minister of the newly established Methodist church, who was well aware of arousals of the flesh.

The summer of George's ride into the inland, when his desire was fresh and new and needing to be slaked regularly, was particularly hot and he stopped often in the shade of small stands of low trees to drink from his water bag and purge various bodily fluids. Vast amounts of piss and semen were expended into the thirsty summer earth where they sank, seemingly without trace.

The following winter found him on the track back towards Siddon Rock. He was returning home, after searching the small settlements and remote homesteads of the bush and desert, still with no house in which to consummate his marriage with Eliza May Winton. He stopped now and then at small shallow ponds that had formed where he had relieved himself on the outward journey. There winter rain had drawn salt water from the ground – like to like, so to speak: salt from the earth joining with the salt of George's bodily fluids. The water was as salty as the sea, as salty as tears, as salty as Eliza's sweat, which he had yet to taste.

George tied his horse to a dying ghost gum tree at the edge of one of these ponds, wondering at the whiteness of the salt-embalmed trunk that seemed as solid as rock. To take his mind from the heat in his body, and to dissolve images of a dark curtained bedroom, he walked out onto the pond's apparently firm surface. As George was bulky – not fat, but rounded and solid, being in stature like his father's side of the family – the surface soon crumbled under him and left him floundering waist-deep in salty water and mud that sucked him slowly but relentlessly into its depths. As he tried to extricate himself from the mire, George sensed a shadow falling over him and looked up to see the ghost gum leaning towards him, falling in slow motion into the pond. His mind flashed pictures of himself trapped by the heavy tree, pushed into the muddy salt water and held until he drowned. He screamed, and tried to get out of the way of the falling tree, but the water was too shallow to allow him to swim and too deep for him to run, and he knew he was going to die.

As he struggled in the grip of the pond, a rope dropped in front of him. George grasped it eagerly and wrapped it around his wrist. The stranger at the other end of the rope helped George to firm ground, where the ghost gum stood sedately upright with his horse tied to it.

George was in two minds about being rescued. The sensibilities brought from England by his father had not been established in George, who had grown up in the roughness of settlement. The rude culture had denied him the spiritual enquiry and good manners that had infused the renaissance soul of Henry in the library at Greater Wickton, so when a stranger pulled him from a shallow pond he was less than gracious, managing a muttered, *Thanks, I was quite all right.*

Yeah, I could see that, the stranger said, and set about lighting a fire. While George's clothes dried, he talked with the man, as passing strangers do. On hearing of his needs, George's rescuer said that he knew someone who knew where there was an abandoned house that might be for sale. *Go back due north about three miles,* he said. *Turn left at the bloodwood tree with the eagle's nest and you should find him after about ten minutes' ride – a trot, not a gallop. If you don't, whistle like thi*s . . . he held his cupped hands to his mouth and produced two notes, like the shrilling of a ship's bosun's whistle. Then he scooped salty water to douse the fire and rode off.

Ten minutes after he had turned left at the bloodwood George could see no house, nor any sign that there was anything around him except reddish earth and mallee scrub. He put his hands to his mouth and then pulled them away. *What a fool!* he said aloud, and his words drifted off. He held his cupped hands to his mouth again and, feeling very glad there was no-one to see him, blew as he had been shown.

The sound that emerged seemed louder and shriller than that of the man who had pulled him from the salt lake. It blasted the stillness of the bush with a force that shivered the thin trunks of the mallee and died quickly as it faded into the trees. *What a fool!* he said again, but as he turned his horse to resume his ride home to Siddon Rock, walking through the scrub was a man who waved at him to stop and then stood silently waiting.

George cleared his throat. *I need a house*, he said, and the words stumbled over each other in their haste to tell the story. *I want to marry Eliza May Winton she won't marry me until I have a house for her a man back there at the salt pond said you'd know where there's one. I'm George Aberline.*

The man nodded. *Yup.* He stuck out his hand and George leaned down from his horse to shake it. *You can know me as Beatty. Lazarus Beatty,* and he started off, with a jerk of his head for George to follow. Not fifty yards from the faint track they stopped, and Lazarus Beatty moved cautiously forward to where the land dropped away in an unexpected precipice. *A bloke could fall over this cliff and do himself some damage,* he said. George dismounted and looked down into a deep gully, to what appeared to be a village of small cottages built with no plan as to streets or placement. *Well,* he said. *Well now, you'd never know anyone lived way out here.*

Lazarus Beatty gave a sharp crack of laughter. *Hah. They don't. These are all from the goldfields.* He lowered himself to the ground and sat back on one heel. *I moved some. Thought I could sell them somewhere. Other people left the gold towns and thought they'd take their house with them – you know how hard it is to get building materials out here – and then got sick of lugging it along.* As he spoke he rolled shaggy tobacco into a small piece of paper.

George waited, thinking there was more to tell. After a minute or two he cleared his throat and asked diffidently, *So why are they here? There's nothing for miles around.*

The man shrugged and lit the ragged cigarette. *Why not here? It's as good a place as any. D' ya want one of 'em or not?*

Oh yes, George said, *most definitely.*

Slipping and sliding on loose dirt and small rocks that rolled down into the gully, Lazarus Beatty led George down the steep slope to the houses. At first he walked with George through the buildings, but as the inspection lengthened into hours he sat on the verandah of a well-built bungalow, propping himself against the wall.

George found himself full of doubt and indecision. How could he select just one house for Eliza May? They all seemed eminently suitable. All had bedrooms and kitchens, and what more could one wish for. He was drawn at first to one, then another. This one had a large verandah; that one, more rooms. This one had strong timber floors that were fast and solid even after the journey from the goldfields; that one was laid with carpet.

George envisioned the firm little face of Eliza May framed by those honey-coloured curls, and understood that a decision must be made, and that it must be the right decision for it would determine the course of his life. He wondered if he could take a selection of the houses for Eliza May to choose the one she liked best. But what to do then with those left over?

As he contemplated the sorry-looking houses scattered through the bush, their walls and roofs sagging with the abandonment of the unloved, George was in despair. *It's no use*, he thought, *I don't know what to do*. He turned to walk away from it all, but the thought of a life without Eliza May made him turn back.

Now, instead of the array of dishevelled derelicts dropped higgledy-piggledy in the barren gully, he saw a gravelled road flanked on either side by green and shady trees quite unlike those of the surounding bush. Behind the trees the houses formed neat rows, each a good distance from the other and centred on its own piece of land. Every house glowed with pride, cleaned and painted in fresh colours: green trimmed with white, a blue roof shielding sparkling white walls, or a creamy colour with deep red window-frames and eaves. There were hammocks and cane chairs filled with comfortable cushions on wide verandahs, and around each house were gardens overflowing with bright flowers and cool greenery.

George walked along the road, stopping to read the signs that were in front of every house: *For Sale. Contact George H. Aberline, Realtor*, they read, each and every one. The blood of English traders stirred in his veins and sent a passionate surge to his heart. *Do you think we could move all these houses if I took the lot?* he asked Lazarus Beatty.

No worries, mate, Lazarus Beatty replied, *just leave it to me*.

So the deal was done, and Lazarus Beatty somehow organised thirty-nine bullock teams, with drays and drivers.

Where they had come from in this empty place George had no idea, but there they were, waiting to go.

In payment, Lazarus Beatty agreed to accept a small amount on account from George, with the balance to be paid whenever he asked for it, at any time in the future.

As the teams loaded with the houses waited to move off, Lazarus Beatty picked up his blanket roll and held out his hand to George. They shook hands and George asked, *What happens if I don't have the money when you come for it?* but with absolute confidence that this would not be so.

You'll be right, mate, Lazarus Beatty said. *Don't worry, you'll be able to pay, one way or another.* He turned towards the inland. After a few steps he called over his shoulder, *After all, there's always your farm, your wife, and your soul.*

George laughed, and raised his arm ready to signal the teams to move on. *I'll see you sometime then,* he said, and when he dropped his arm the noise of the bullockies and lumbering drays drowned out any reply Lazarus Beatty may have made.

George navigated from memory and by following the chain of small salt ponds that he had seeded with his bodily fluids at the beginning of his quest. This resulted in a somewhat winding journey, but the houses on the drays pulled by bullocks followed him sedately wherever he led, and gradually he made his way to Siddon Rock and Eliza May Winton.

The long, slow days with the bullocks allowed George time to think, and the thing that filled his mind was the vision in the gully. *Just like my father,* he thought. *Like the one that sent him here to find the butterfly.* Then he'd laugh, knowing that no such butterfly could ever be found; that it was an illusion, a story. At least his own vision was of some use. He'd not spend his life under a tree on a rock. He, George Aberline, was going to be the most successful businessman the district would ever see, and between the sale of these houses following so placidly behind him, the farm that he would develop, and a business that would hire out bullock teams with drays, he'd be the richest man in town, and well able to start his own dynasty.

With the thirty-nine houses in an orderly line behind him, George rode slowly into Siddon Rock, his calm demeanour showing nothing of the trials of the journey. He parked them on the open ground opposite the pub, then walked confidently to the Winton's cottage where Eliza May waited for him.

The large selection of houses sent Eliza May Winton quite out of character when she had to choose one. Eventually she eliminated all except one with large, high-ceilinged rooms and the one with the verandah where Lazarus Beatty had waited for George. *We'll have both*, George said, and took them to their new farm just two miles out of the town. There, with the help of a round-up of brothers, he joined them together into the large and impressive farmhouse that stands there now.

While George was away, Eliza May had taken up land not far from the small salt lake that was already forming at

George's first stop on the outward journey. When George told her that he intended to open a stock and station agency as well as run the farm, Eliza was delighted that she had chosen land so close to town. Eliza would, of course, oversee the farm operations if necessary while George worked the agency.

Eliza May named the house 'Aberwin' to signify the joining of the families of Aberline and Winton into one; but to everyone else it was known as the Two Mile, so that gradually even Eliza May referred to it as such, and 'Aberwin' faded from the town's memory.

As for the other houses, George persuaded the newly formed Siddon Rock Council to let him have land behind the hotel. Thirty-seven houses were set in their own blocks, as he had seen in his vision, although the blast of summer heat and lack of water killed the street trees George planted, and he never did replace them. The sales of the houses, together with the ongoing business of used dray and cart trading and bullock team hire, and the newly established stock and station agency, proved him as a solid businessman of the town.

When the Council asked him if he would like to name the street where his houses were set, George called it Whistler's Way, and just shrugged when asked why such a strange name.

No-one remembered when Granna arrived.

Over time many of the Aberline clan tried to place

her with their forebears. The problem was that it was difficult to say just where she fitted in the family, or if indeed she did. There were old photographs of Aberline gatherings where a likeness could seem to be hers; but when asked where she was among the fading images, Granna's favourite answer was, *Youth is a disguise. You can't expect to recognise me in there.* There were also letters with a vague reference to 'her' or 'the woman', but there never was an identifying name or anything specific; say, for instance 'so-and-so's daughter' or 'at such-and-such event with her husband, so-and-so'.

Others attempted to prove she was just a ghost, or a figment of the imagination. But there she was, driving into town with Eliza May or, down the generations, with the wife of whichever Aberline was in possession of the Two Mile; and try as they might she would not be reduced to a wraith or a remembrance.

Then there were those who thought that Granna could have been one of Henry Aberline's sightseeing women, one of those who came to talk with him and were captivated by the romantic idea of natural love under his tree on the rock. *If she was a very young woman then*, they said, *and is a very, very old woman now, maybe this could be the case.* But to say at what time Granna had been a young woman – if indeed she had ever been – was impossible, as there was no town memory of this.

The favourite story was that Granna had arrived at the Two Mile in one of the houses that George Aberline brought in for Eliza May. After all, who knew where they had been before George found them. But in that case, where had

Granna been for all those months while the houses were being joined together and renovated? No-one could say.

So nothing could be proved. To those indiscreet enough to enquire her age Granna would reply, *I'm as old as my tongue and a little older than my teeth*, and then flash a big smile that displayed teeth as white and pearly as a child's. If they persisted she said that it was way too long ago and she didn't remember.

But no-one believed that.

The bestowing of a name on the nameless woman – for she never did give a name for herself – was accidental.

When George Aberline drove Eliza May to the house after their wedding on a cold and overcast winter's afternoon, they saw smoke rising from the kitchen chimney. They rushed inside, there to find the nameless woman preparing the evening meal. The fire glowed in the kitchen stove, the smell of freshly baked bread wafted through the house, and a leg of lamb crackled and browned as it roasted in the oven. Eliza May smiled at the woman. *How lovely to walk into the warmth*, she said.

George, however, protested loudly, throwing open the door and demanding that she remove herself immediately from their home. The woman ignored him and addressed herself to Eliza May. *You're going to need all the help you can get*, she said.

As the woman spoke, Eliza May heard, as if in the next room, many children calling out and crying. There were the sounds of arguments and fighting, mixed with the clang of slow-tolling bells. The voice of her new husband echoed strangely: *I don't have it,* he said. *You'll just have to wait.* A man answered, someone she did not know. *We shook on it, mate. If you can't pay in money, then it will have to be the other way.*

What did you shake on? Eliza May demanded of George. *George, what was it?*

George looked confused. *I don't know what you mean, I've been shaking hands all day.* He took her arm solicitously and tried to help her to a chair. *It's been a long day. You must be exhausted with all the excitement.*

Eliza May waved him away. *There's nothing wrong with me,* she said. *And the woman stays. Obviously she can cook, and I need someone to help in the house. So she'll always be here.*

And so she was.

Eliza May called the woman Nanna, a name containing within it acknowledgement of her assistance in the home and deference to her unknown age. One of the many children born by Eliza May thought Nanna was her grandmother, and started to call her Grandma. When Eliza explained that this was not so, the child became confused and welded the two names together immutably, so that Granna had, in the mind of the Aberline family, and eventually of the town, always been so called.

Granna said that the name was as good as any and served its purpose, which was to make it easy to call her from another room.

Macha Connor's father was Charles Henry George Aberline, great-grandson of Henry Aberline who had inadvertently caused the founding of Siddon Rock and the inheritance of the Aberline sadness, grandson of George Henry who had carted thirty-nine houses to form the township of Siddon Rock, and son of Thomas Henry, farmer and owner of two large properties, one of which was the Two Mile.

Charlie succumbed to the melancholia of the Aberlines particularly early. He walked into the desert two days after his marriage to Brigid Connor – the daughter of the Irish couple who worked on his father's farm – in the Church of the Immaculate Conception.

Some in the town said it was the vying forces within his nature that sent him away. It was to be expected that a man could not live with the profoundly physical expectations imposed by life on the land when such a sadness of spirit was present. Others, of the Protestant persuasion, muttered that it was the shame of being forced by his new bride to make his vows in the Roman church; and yet others whispered that he had a woman who lived on the goldfields.

Those who knew the family talked about breed-lines, and how the sadness had arrived in Charlie from both parents, being aunt and nephew as they were. Aberline men remembered their ancestors' early departure from this earth and had a brief shiver of doubt about their own seeming immortality, but this was quickly dispersed by the dry air, heat and exertion of working their land.

After Charlie disappeared from the Two Mile, Brigid walked for a full day around the boundary of the farm. By the time she had returned to the farmhouse she knew that she would never work on someone else's farm again. She would not go back to washing other people's dirty dishes nor help out in other farmers' shearing sheds. She owned this land, and she would hold it against all blandishments by the Aberline clan. And so she did, holding them away with the tough spirit learnt in the battleground of the schoolyard so recently left, and the inheritance of her mother's stories. *Where would I go?* she said. *What would I do? This is mine now, and I'll farm it. You can help or not – it's not important.* But when she found she was pregnant, Brigid went to Charlie's father, Thomas Henry. *I'm carrying your son's son*, she said bluntly. *You can help me, or you can make it hard. Granna is here to help in the house, but I need to hire a farmhand for the heavy things. You have the money. I can't imagine what the town would say if you refused help to your son's pregnant wife.* And so Thomas Aberline paid for Mellor Mackintosh to live in the shearer's quarters at the Two Mile.

With the advent of Mellor, Brigid had time to prepare for her child's birth. Her own mother, even on her long death-bed, had told her stories of her Irish heritage, taking the child Brigid to a time when Ireland grew out of conflict and courage. *Your name means 'strong'*, she told the child. *And strong you must be.* Now Brigid spent the evenings reading books of Gaelic history and mythology, for she was convinced that her line of Connor was that of Cuchulain the Champion of Ireland, and that she had the blood of kings and warriors to pass on to her son.

When the baby was born Granna wrapped her in cotton blankets and placed her on her side in a wooden slatted cot. Brigid sat watching the baby, stunned that this child was not the solid son she expected, but instead a small, thin girl who had not yet made a vocal welcome to the world. *What am I to call you?* she said. The child's mouth began to work and Brigid went to pick her up, thinking she needed to be fed, but from the cot came a clear bell-like sound of two notes in a minor key. *Maayyy chaaa* rang around the room.

Brigid stopped in wonder. *Holy Mother of God*, she said, making the sign of the cross over the cot. *Holy Mother of God, what do I have here?*

Maayyy chaaaa. The baby sang more strongly, the purity of the notes ringing out across the house-yard. Granna, who was throwing handfuls of wheat for a scratching of scrawny chooks, dropped the bucket and ran to the room. There, Brigid was on her knees, praying loudly with her hands over her ears. *Do get up, Brigid*, she said sharply. *The child is merely telling her name.*

Is it Marsha, then? Brigid was dubious, this not being a name she had any liking for. And for a third time the notes sounded:

Maaaaaaayy chaaaaaaaaaa, and this time there was a hint of impatience in the space between the two perfect notes.

Maychar, I think. Granna's ear was more attuned to the unhearable.

Brigid ran to her books of Gaelic mythology, followed by Granna. *There's a warrior woman named Macha.*

It means Goddess. Do you think that's it? They looked dubiously at the skinny baby. Then another two notes rang out. *Laaaaa leeeeeee.*

    I think, Granna said, *that her name is Macha Lalie.* And a small smile came to the face of Brigid's child, who was Henry Aberline's great-great-granddaughter, but with the blood of Cuchulain the Champion of Ireland, from her mother.

When Macha Connor was five years old and went to school, in the tradition of name-changing by children, she was immediately called May. But this name was too reminiscent of an English spring, was too sweet and delicate for the strong farm-child, and it was soon abandoned.

CHAPTER THREE

MEN'S BUSINESS

There comes a time when we have to recognise ourselves in the mirror.

NOT LONG AFTER MACHA CONNOR CAME HOME FROM WAR, Young George Aberline – who was still called Young George even at the age of forty-five – had the thought to mine the lake for salt. This was triggered by a discussion with his sister-in-law Brigid Connor, who complained of the encroachment of the salt onto her land, and pointed out that the lake, of late, seemed to have less water in winter and a firmer crust in summer.

He raised the possibility with Brigid first, saying *You're good with figures, Brig, how about making a business with me?*

Not interested, Brigid said. *Enough on my hands, what with the farm and Macha home. But if you ever want a bit of a help . . . I know you're not so good at the arithmetic side of things.* They both recalled, but didn't say, that Brigid had done all Young George's sums for him when they sat side-by-side at school.

Might as well make something from the friggin' stuff, Young George said to Sinclair Johnson, who was writing an article about the possible venture for the local paper. *Ain't no use to God or man, otherwise.* And from then on salt became the passion and obsession of Young George Aberline.

No good will come of such a hare-brained scheme, the town said. *Once an Aberline steps a foot off the farm into business, there's trouble for sure.* Granna, when she read of Young George's venture in the *District Examiner & Journal*, remembered the visitor to Young George's grandfather, George Henry Aberline, on the day before he walked into the salt lake. Although at the time there had been the usual speculation about the visitor and his role in George Henry's death, if any, Granna was the only one who knew that Lazarus Beatty had come for the repayment of a loan made on a handshake, and that George Henry had had trouble recalling this. She burnt the *Examiner* and held her tongue.

Young George, nothing if not thorough in his research, sailed to England on the *Orion* with his son David. They made their way to the Midlands where George had written ahead for an appointment with the manager of the Thompson Salt Works at Northwich, not far from Greater Wickton.

When they registered at the hotel, the clerk looked at their signed names. *Aberline*, he said. *There's a lot of them around here. An old family, it is. You're here to look up relations, then?*

Young George shrugged it away. *Business*, he said curtly. *We're here on business.*

Not really interested in all that, David said. *Leave it to the women.*

David and Young George walked around the town while they waited for the meeting at Thompson's. David ran his hand along the rough stone walls of a row of terraced houses. *Just think of what's holding these places up. Just think of all that dust that's been hanging around for centuries – all those old people and trees turned into dust and stuck in the walls. Maybe there's even some old dinosaur dust stuck in there. No wonder the Poms are a pale-looking lot, breathing all that old stuff all the time.*

Dust is just dust, Young George said; he wasn't sure about young David at times. He thought too much about things that didn't matter. *And there's enough effin' dust at home to last a lifetime for the world. So why don't you stop thinking about dust and start thinking about salt. That's what's going to make us – salt – not bloody dust. Salt's important. It's been used for centuries.* George had indeed been doing his reading. *And it's needed to cure fish, to make things like Roquefort cheese, and corned beef is called corned because of the small bits of salt, or corns, that are used to cure it.* Young George was in full flight. *And flamingos are pink because their diet is shrimps and worms from salt ponds. And . . . and there's a salt mine in Poland that's also a church.*

Well, said David, *you don't have to make a blasted speech about it. Get off your high horse.* He started to walk off, but turned back to Young George. *But I wouldn't mind seeing that. The church. But all that other stuff, we don't do that in Siddon Rock . . . except the corned beef. Sybil Barber does a great corned beef.*

We've gotta get it out of Siddon Rock. Young George was getting testy.

David wondered if the weeks on a ship bouncing about on water had shaken up his father more than he realised. *I suppose we could go to the port and see the fisheries about using Siddon Rock salt for salting fish, then. There's three ports, surely some of the fishing people would be interested. We could teach them how to salt fish, if we had to.*

Now you're thinking, Young George said. *That's the spirit!*

At the Thompson Salt Works, Young George and David were impressed with the generosity of the manager, who spent two days taking them with him on his normal rounds. They walked the salt-beds, asking questions and writing the answers in notebooks. They discussed the wherefores and hows of extraction with the foremen and even went so far as to talk to the men as they worked the routine of salt-making. But the Aberlines quickly realised that this method was not for them, as a large supply of firewood or coke was needed to heat the brine. The Siddon Rock district being what it was, with low scrubby bush and no tall timber, this was impossible.

The manager suggested that they visit the coast of Brittany in France where, he assured them, salt was harvested by the natural method of letting water into ponds, which were then dried and scraped. This, he thought, would probably suit their needs better.

With a letter of introduction from the manager of Thompson's, Young George and David took passage to France on a turbulent day when the waters of the English Channel heaved and rocked under the ferry. Young George stayed below in the lounge with the other passengers, and David was the only person on the open deck, exhilarating in the wildness. *What a place*, he thought as the wind and rain whipped at him, *what a bloody magnificent place.* At that moment David Aberline thought that maybe Siddon Rock, the farm, and the dead water of the salt lake were not for him.

In France, Young George and David made their way to Brittany and the saltworks outside the ancient town of Guérande. They were amazed at the drained swamps that were divided into channels leading to concentration ponds, where the sun evaporated the water from its salt. *If it wasn't for the sea there*, David said, *and if you squint a bit, we could be in Siddon Rock. And look out there. That could be the silo.*

Young George shaded his eyes against the glare from the salt pans and peered out to sea. In the far distance was a tall, round, stone building that looked as if it was rising from the surface of a mirage. He was uneasy, unable to reconcile these things that he felt were out of their place, which he knew was Siddon Rock. Young George turned away and concentrated on the mechanics of the crystallising pans, watching how the salt was raked into rows to drain. *We can do this*, he thought. *The salt lake is perfect for this.*

As for David Aberline, his new understanding of the vastness of the world was crystallised on the Brittany coast, and he knew that the call of the world outside Siddon Rock would eventually become too strong to resist.

The first thing Young George did when he got home was go to the State and Farmers' Bank, to arrange a loan for the new business of Geo. Aberline & Son Minerals. When the manager began to explain the terms and conditions, Young George impatiently took the pen from his hand and signed the papers. *It's done*, he said. *Now we go to work.*

You do realise that the farm is mortgaged to the business, the manager said. *Yeah, of course*, Young George called back through the closing door, *there won't be a problem.*

Every evening at exactly six-thirty, Alistair Meakins double-checked the locks on the doors and windows of Meakins' Haberdashery and Ladies & Men's Apparel. He placed his hat on his head and the day's takings in a small cloth bag which he tied to his braces, buttoning his coat over it. Then he walked down the back lane to his home.

On Saturday night Alistair would celebrate the end of the working week, and go to the hotel for two whisky and sodas and a chat with Marge Redall. He liked the cloud of tiny shapes that surrounded Marge like blue haze, and found her loudness and warmth a tonic.

Every other night Alistair turned on the wireless as he made his meal, listening to the seven o'clock news broadcast, and then settling for an hour or two of reading. He was particularly fond of stories of European and Asian cultures, and of histories of fashion and trade, and would pore over a large world atlas for hours, imagining what it would be like to live in the various countries. In winter he sat in his lounge-room close to a fire of mallee roots, for inland winter nights have a chill that can bite to the bone. In summer the back verandah was his favourite place, being deep, and greenly secluded from neighbours by a thick grapevine on a latticed trellis. Wire screens protected against mosquitoes and flies, and there was a standing lamp beside Alistair's chair for reading in the cool of the night.

This night, though, the night Macha Connor came home from war, Alistair deviated from his well-established pattern and placed himself in a story that he thought was all his own.

After he washed the dishes and put them away, Alistair pulled the window blinds to below the edge of the sill and turned off all the lights in the house, except that in the bathroom. There, he covered the window with black material, tacking it in place with drawing-pins so that no light would be seen from the outside. *They did this in London during the blitz*, he thought, *so no light would give them away*. When he was certain that his concealment was complete, he went into his bedroom where he lit three candles, opened a large trunk at the foot of the bed, and laid out the contents.

Alistair took off his coat and slipped the braces from his shoulders. His shirt, socks and underwear went into the dirty-clothes basket, and the trousers clipped into a wooden trouser holder so that the crease-line fell into place. He took a smallish wooden box from the trunk and carried this and a candle to the bathroom, where he lit the woodchip heater next to the bath, feeding the flames with pieces of paper and twigs. When the water in the heater started to steam Alistair caught some in a basin, then mixed a thick lather in his shaving mug and lavished this on his face and chest. He stropped the cut-throat razor against a leather strap hanging behind the door, and when it was shining-sharp drew it carefully over his cheeks, chin and chest until there was no sign of a dark shadow.

Alistair washed the razor in the basin then stropped it again before heating it in the gush of boiling water pouring into the bath. He smoothed a fresh lather onto his stomach and around his scrotum until the pubic hair was well covered, then held his penis gingerly between thumb and finger while carefully manipulating the razor until his genitals lay against a barren landscape. The light hair on his legs disappeared with a few swift strokes. He hesitated about trying to remove the small vee of hair growing at the base of his spine, eventually deciding against it with the thought of trying to explain to Doctor Allen how he had got a razor cut to a buttock.

When he was smooth-skinned, apart from the spinal vee, Alistair shook lavender bath crystals into the tub and turned off the overhead light. By the glow of the single candle he lowered himself into the fragrant, steaming water. There he lay blissfully, with pale legs and rounded belly floating above the lavender bubbles until it cooled to tepid, when he stepped out and wrapped a towel around himself.

Alistair turned on the main light and opened the small wooden box. In it were items that he had seen in the *Women's Weekly*. He explained in his letters to the manufacturers that he had a business with a small and exclusive clientele for which he required samples of quality make-up, and they always sent back what he requested.

Alistair started with the toenails, and applied *Fire-Engine Red* nail polish, holding the toes apart with small bundles of cottonwool torn from a roll. As the polish dried he applied to his soft and steam-shined face: Max Factor Pancake foundation, colour *Naturelle*, stroked on with a dampened sponge until no natural skin could be seen on face or throat; Lournay Face Powder, colour *Peche*, dusted over the foundation with a large and fluffy powder-puff. Next, he dabbed his fingertip into a small pot of rouge and smudged this below his cheekbone, smoothing it up and out so that the colour blended with no visible demarcation. Then came the final touch – Helena Rubinstein *Deep Velvet* lipstick, best described as a delicious cyclamen with a red background. Alistair usually had trouble with keeping the line of the lip, but this night perfect lips shaped immediately.

Back in the bedroom, by the light of the candles reflecting in the long mirror next to the dressing table, Alistair opened a gold cardboard box that had a handwritten card tucked in the ribbon tying it. *For Allison* it read, and when Alistair felt the sinuous flow of silk on his fingers he was pleased that she had decided to buy the elegant black panties, matching petticoat and suspender belt that he had made for her during the war. This box had been put aside for her at Meakins' Haberdashery and Ladies & Men's Apparel until she was ready to collect it. Unlike the garments of the *La'Mour* label he had created at that time from cheaper celanese material, these bespoke garments were handmade from quality silk woven from single threads: the feather-light float of the petticoat showed that there was no doubling or crossing of threads together.

Alistair touched the garment to his cheek to feel its exquisite texture, and as he did so he saw a black thread detach from the hem and float towards the covered window. Alistair cautiously opened the blind a little, and knelt down to watch its flight. The thread drifted into the bright night, a fine, black cursive trail against the whiteness of a full moon as it wafted this way and that, before turning towards the coast. He continued to hold the half-slip, expecting it to unravel as the thread grew longer behind the errant strand, but it stayed full and soft in his hands.

Alistair stood at the window watching the thread fly across the Southern Ocean, and then turn north, up the west coast of Africa to Europe – was it to France or Italy? Maybe Spain? He rather hoped the first as he'd like to see Paris, particularly Montmartre, but the thread hovered, coursing this way and that. Suddenly it reared up, as if sniffing the air, and dashed away towards the east. *Of course.* Alistair laughed out loud. *The Silk Road! It's found the Silk Road. It's going home.*

Across the deserts and mountains of Asia flew the silken thread – Iran, Afghanistan, Pakistan, Nepal: the images flashed by so fast that Alistair did not have time to identify each one separately – and into China, where it went directly to a city somewhere in the interior. It found a small cottage where a young woman pushed a bobbin through gossamer-fine cross-threads, her hands so fast they became a blur as she wove the silk into fabric. It circled the woman, who did not notice it, then drifted out of the cottage, across the city to a stone building at its edge, and into a room lined with many shelves on which lay bamboo baskets. The thread floated down into one of these with a soft swaying motion, and Alistair lost sight of it. An old woman tended these baskets, checking their contents one by one as she crooned softly in a Chinese dialect, and Alistair heard her lullaby:

> *Sleep my precious babies*
> *mother's here to care for you*
> *hide your tiny selves from harm*
> *grow the wings to fly away*
> *and thread for ladies' silken robes*
> *you will make today.*

As Alistair stood at the window holding the petticoat in his hands sadness touched him and he envied the garment's completeness.

So here it is, Alistair said to himself, *Allison's undies are made by a grub in China.*

Alistair rolled black nylons up his legs and fastened them into the suspender belt. He looked up and caught sight of himself in the mirror. *Allison really likes quality things, doesn't she?* he said to the image. *Such a very special person. It's so good that I'm able to find the very best for her, through the shop.* A small smile quirked at the corners of his lips, and he sang as he tucked his genitals, and eased into the panties, half-slip and camisole:

> *I'm gonna dance with the dolly with the hole in*
> * her stocking*
> *While her knees keep on knockin'*
> *And her toes keep on rockin',*
> *Gonna dance with the dolly with the hole in her*
> * stocking*
> *Gonna dance by the light of the moon.*

From the very back of the wardrobe Alistair took two frocks: a black *crêpe de chine* with bugle beads edging the neckline, and a deep red rayon printed with pale blue flowers. Alistair shook them out and looked at them critically, comparing them with the elegant silver-grey Dior creation depicted on the wall of the fitting room of Meakins' Haberdashery and Ladies & Men's Apparel. *I think we should make Allison a new dress,* he said with a little sigh. *This red thing is only fit for the rag-bag, and this* – he patted the other disparagingly – *is really outdated. But it'll have to do for tonight.*

Alistair unfastened a row of buttons and stepped into the frock. He smoothed the skirt over his plump hips,

70

slipped his feet into high-heeled pumps and screwed gold and pearl earrings onto reddening earlobes. Lastly, he snuffed all but one candle, leaving the room in a flickering twilight with dark shadows hanging at the corners. Then he took the hatbox from the wardrobe shelf and opened it.

Alistair knew the hat well. He had, after all, commissioned its making by the French milliners, Etablissements Werlé, Créateur de chapeaux féminins. Only the best for the best, Alistair had thought at the time, and had a vision of a small, head-hugging suit hat of crushed velvet with full netting over the face; black, to go with either the black frock or the red. He was surprised then, as he sketched the hat, that the drawing on the paper in front of him was nothing at all like his original idea. The drawing had a mind of its own and no matter where he placed the marks on the paper, the same design appeared: a flat-crowned hat with a wide, drooping brim. He threw the sheet of paper in the bin and started again, annoyed that his drawing skill had left him; but the same hat was drawn. Eventually he shrugged. *Must be the one she wants*, he thought, and mailed it off to Paris together with a covering letter detailing instructions as to delivery.

Some months later a plain brown box with French stamps arrived at the Siddon Rock post office. Alistair's fingers itched to open the parcel, but he contained his excitement until he got home that evening, tearing away the wrapping the minute he shut the door behind him. Inside the brown packaging was the trademark silver and maroon striped hatbox of Ets. Werlé; he lifted the lid and reverently opened the tissue paper packing.

Taking the hat from its box he was amazed, for this was not the design he had sent. *How strange*, he said out loud. *How most peculiar that a firm with such a reputation would send the wrong hat.*

It was indeed not the pattern Alistair had sent: this hat had a high sloping crown, with a deep brim turned up at one side and held in place by a large stick-pin. The pin itself had a simple decorative shape at its top that suggested the stylised wings of a butterfly, which were encrusted with gold stones. When the pin was thrust through to hold the brim against the crown, the wings lay flat along the turn-up. But it was the material of the hat that was a puzzlement to Alistair, for it was nothing he had ever seen before. Neither felt nor velvet, the material was firm but luxuriously soft, and as he held it up to the rather dull light in his kitchen, the colour alternated from a rich maroon-red to black, and he was quite unable to determine which was the main colour. It was a glorious concoction, no doubt, but it was not what Alistair had asked for; it was not what he had told Allison he had ordered, and he wondered what she would think of it. He put it back in its box, ready to take to the shop for her to make a decision.

Now, Alistair carried the hat and a small handbag with a chain handle to the chair on the verandah. There he sat with them on his lap.

Around him the sounds of Siddon Rock were magnified by the stillness of the night, and confused as to direction. The dull thump of the power station – not noticed in the everyday course of things – was a rhythmic background to the clinking of dishes being washed and the snuffles and occasional bark of dogs in the street. Now and then the faint cry of a plover drifted in from the paddocks, or sudden music from a radio blasted out as a station was changed. A motorbike roared into town and Alistair wondered if Fatman Aberline was going to the pub, and why wasn't he with his cousin Macha on this, her first night home. He, Alistair, would have been caring for her, making sure she was welcomed home with warmth and love.

Slowly, slowly the sounds of the town diminished. The dinner dishes were dried and put away, the radio turned off as the owner went to bed, the motorbike noisily left town, and the thump of the power station decreased to a soft hum and then silence as Abe Simmons shut it down for the night. Now all that was heard was a single mourning plover and an occasional dying fall of the yelp-howl of a dingo.

Slowly, slowly Alistair Meakins stood up, walked easily to the mirror at the side of the kitchen door, and put on the hat. He spun so that the skirt of the frock swirled in dark waves at his knees, then he smiled at the mirror. *Hello Allison*, he said, *that is a glorious hat. And look where the pin sits, those wings are just perfect at the side front. Are you ready, darling? Tonight we become brave.*

Allison stepped off the verandah onto hard earth that held the day's heat, walking lightly, nearly on tiptoe, to stop the clink of high heels on the gravelly ground. At the gate in the back fence she slid the bolt, looked both ways and then walked up the back lane. She turned into the side street, stopped at the post office corner, and drew in a shaky breath. *Come on, girl,* she said. *If Macha Connor can do it, so can you.* She adjusted her hat slightly downwards and stepped around the corner into Wickton Street.

Allison expected only the beam of the bright moon in the street. The wavering light that met her made her press back against the wall of the post office, waiting for some clue to tell her what had happened. There was no sound and no-one in the street and, when the pounding panic that caught her breathing quietened, Allison realised that Abe Simmons had forgotten to turn off the street lights when he closed down the generator. Now they were pulsating from dim to bright as they pulled the power from the storage batteries.

She hesitated, wondering if she should go back, but gathered herself. *Don't rush,* she said to herself. *Just one step after another. There's no-one around, so just take your time.*

Allison crept past the darkened post office and the closed window of the telephone exchange, dark now and silent of ringing bells. Through the thick brick walls she felt the restless sleep of Tommy Hinks dreaming of fame and fortune. She knew that Tommy saved the extra money he got for working the night shift, waiting to move to the excitement of the capital.

At Barber's Butchery & Bakery, a cursory glance showed a display cabinet empty of meat. At the back of the shop she could see the ghostly shape of a cloth-covered tray that she knew was the next day's bread: already the cloth was rising as the yeast worked its magic.

More confident now, Allison paused to look in the window of Meakins' Haberdashery and Ladies & Men's Apparel. There she saw floral cotton frocks on two plaster models standing in one corner, and a thigh-length coat with a swinging back over a long, straight skirt on another that stood alone. Allison adjusted her hat slightly in the reflection and swung her skirt. *Don't worry, m'dears*, she said, *you're perfect for the town.*

She smiled and walked on down the empty street with the pulsing light. Her tentative walk became a slight sway, and then a swing as she went past the Farmers' Co-op, past the pub and the State and Farmers' Bank until she reached the Shire Hall and Council Offices at the end of the main street. Any further and she would be on the path that led past the silo and up the rock. Here she paused, and the flickering light behind her glowed more brightly, reflecting in the tall frosted glass doors of the hall. Allison swung neatly on one foot – a perfect turn – and paused for a moment.

Now the street was longer and wider with shifting shadows at either side changing the shapes of Wickton Street's shops and buildings. From Meakins' Haberdashery and Ladies' & Men's Apparel a strong, steady glow brightened the central area of the street from the shops to the war memorial, which trembled, appearing shorter for a moment then returning to its normal shape. Allison could swear there was water cascading from the top, and the pepper trees at the edge of the railway station-yard looked like willows drooping over a tranquil river.

Allison laughed out loud. *Yes*, she said, *what fun*. She saucily swung her handbag on its chain and stepped out, confident now that if she saw any man he would tip his hat politely to a beautiful woman. She drew level with the pub, and for a moment the façade changed from timber boards to solid grey stone blocks with wide windows. Allison pressed close to the window-pane, peering around the 'Railway and Traveller's Hotel' written on the glass, and could clearly see the interior where tables were set at a discreet distance from each other and covered with white damask. Attentive waiters hovered solicitously over the diners, pouring wine, shaking napkins. In the open kitchen white-hatted chefs were busy. As she watched, a man in a tall chef's hat and carrying a large book entered the back of the restaurant through a door that he locked after him. *The Executive Chef*, Allison thought. *Maybe tomorrow's menu is written in the book. Or the provisions required at the markets. He will, of course, shop for these himself*. The man looked up and saw Allison watching. He walked towards her, his face lit up with a strange smile. The intimate interior light in the room made his one brown eye glow but the other, blue, eye was cold and empty. Allison turned away quickly, pleased that she had been acknowledged.

Is it Rome or Paris? Allison asked herself. *Not London, I think. Maybe it's Madrid, it's certainly warm enough.*

Back she went down Wickton Street, Siddon Rock, swinging her skirt and smiling, and all the while the strange light wavered around her. Back past the brightly lit windows of the Farmers' Co-op, devoid of the usual bags of sugar and flour and now stacked high in a display of baroque excess. An impossible pyramid of brown eggs towered over walls of cheeses of all sorts: gruyère, camembert, gorgonzola nestled side by side with bowls of olives, stacks of onions and bright green and red vegetables and grey herbs. The picture it made, Allison said as she walked by without stopping, *should be an exhibit in an art gallery.*

As Allison drew closer to Meakins' Haberdashery and Ladies' & Men's Apparel the light became stronger and began to flash with short and urgent beats, as if caught and reflected in a rotating mirror, urging her on. She refused it, purposefully slowing to a longer, more languorous pace and, as she reached the edge of the display window, paused for a moment before stepping close. From somewhere outside the lights, dogs howled.

Yes, Allison breathed, *oh yes.* There in the window stood a tall, thin model wearing the dress from the photograph on the wall of the dressing room. In splendid isolation the model changed poses, holding each one briefly as if for a fashion photographer. As she moved, the dress took on a life of its own and the full skirt flowed and swayed from a tight bodice cinched at the waist, swirling so that white lace petticoats were exposed under the demure surface of grey faille. Allison trembled, she could see nothing else, just the dress and the posing model; all desire was held in the moment.

This is the House of Dior. This is Avenue Montaigne. This is Paris.

The flashing, pulsing light softened and slowed to an occasional fluctuation, and in the display window the posing Parisienne in the Dior gown faded away, and plaster models wearing Alistair Meakins' choices for the ladies of Siddon Rock appeared in stiff and formal postures. Allison smiled tremulously at them, but found she could not speak to reassure them of their worth.

Quietly now, Allison walked on. At Barber's Butchery & Bakery a *charcuterie* and a *pâtisserie* competed for display space, fading in and out in slow and ever-diminishing ripples; but she merely glanced in the window as she passed. Next door in the telephone exchange Tommy Hicks dreamed an impatient dream of long-legged dancers clothed only in feathers and spangles, as Allison turned the corner into the soft dust and dead grasses of the back lane leading to Alistair's home.

Allison discarded her dusty shoes on the back verandah and went into the closed-up house. She relit the candles in the bedroom, unfastened the long row of buttons on the *crêpe de chine* frock and stepped out of it. Then she removed the hat, and as she put it tenderly into its box the reflected flicker of candlelight in the mirror drew her gaze and she glanced up. There in the glass was a short, soft-looking, middle-aged man with greying hair and garish make-up melting down his face. Black silk underwear, crumpled from the heat of his plump body, cut into the folds of skin on his belly. Allison stood straighter to confront the image but the surface of the mirror fluttered like water under a teasing breeze. From the disturbance emerged the image of a tall, thin woman with straw-coloured hair framing a white mask. The woman raised her arms to the mask, and Allison peered closer to see her face; but when the mask was down, there was no face to see.

In the dark Alistair cried ribbons of make-up into his immaculate bed.

From the shadows of the war memorial Nell watched Allison walk up the street and pause briefly before she made her perfect turn. As she did, all the light in the street gathered around Meakins' Haberdashery and Ladies' & Men's Apparel and Nell could see movement in the display window. The strange light pulsed across the street to where Nell sat, and further to the edge of the railway station-yard. The restive dingoes either side of her whimpered so that Nell put her hand on their heads to reassure them.

As Allison drew closer to the shop the light changed to a throbbing beat and the steps of the war memorial moved beneath the woman and the dogs, becoming broader and wider. A spray of water misted the air, even though there were no clouds in the sky. The dingoes howled in protest at the alteration of their world. *Let's go home, fellas*, Nell said to the dogs. *That Alistair's dreamin' something we don't wanna know about.* But the dingoes had already fled to the safety of Nell's hut in the ancient creek-bed.

Kelpie Crush was always the last to leave the bar. Every night he closed and bolted the doors, picked up glasses, washed them and left them to drain dry. He wiped the bar and threw the towels into the wash-house behind the kitchen. When all was ready for the next day, he would take the key to the Strangers' Room from his pocket and fit it into the lock.

A week or so after he had started at the pub Kelpie Crush spoke to Bluey Redall. *I collect things and they should be away where they can't get damaged,* he said. *The Strangers' Room's not used at all – too dark for anything, with no windows. If I cleaned it up, d'you think I could use it?*

Bluey Redall, anxious to keep such a deft and already popular barman happy, said, *Seeing no bloody strangers ever come to Siddon Rock anyway, you may's well use the room.* Then, remembering that he knew nothing about this bloke except that he was a good barman, added, *And don't go lighting any bloody fires in there either.*

Kelpie Crush seemed to be liked right from the start. Sinclair Johnson, the owner of the *District Examiner & Journal*, who always propped at the street window of the bar so he could keep an eye on the comings and goings in the town, asked the new barman what his name was.

Robert, never called Bob.

Sinclair Johnson looked at the barman's wiry body, dusty-brown colouring and slicked-down hair. *You look like a bloody sheep-dog. A kelpie,* he said. *Should be out there rounding up bloody sheep.* And so Robert Crush became known as Kelpie at the pub, and then through the town, until his original name was forgotten.

The pub regulars also agreed, but out of range of Kelpie's hearing, that it was quite off-putting to talk to the man at times because a bloke didn't know if he was being looked at with the blue eye or the gingery-brown one. Most felt that it was better to stand slightly on the side of the brown eye, which seemed to be less confrontational than the other.

Kelpie blended well with the town. He played hockey on Saturday, where his darting turns of speed and low-lying attacks placed him in the forward line; and football on Sunday. He got to know Harry Best quite well after the little talk about starting a cub scouts pack. Well enough, anyway, to play poker each Tuesday evening with Harry, Sinclair Johnson and Abe Simmons. He joked with the three men that between them they controlled the town – *education, information and power,* he'd say. *Forget the bloody Shire Council, you blokes run the place.*

The thing Kelpie did not discuss with the poker players, or anyone else for that matter, was his collection of moths and insects. Sinclair tried, several times, to draw him out on what he was actually doing with the specimens caught by the cub scouts on their camps near the salt lake, or by other interested people. He'd just shrug it away like a nuisance fly, and once snapped at Sinclair when the newspaperman wanted to do an article about what Kelpie had found out about the local species. *What I do is my business*, he said, and the usually warm gingery-brown eye looked quite cold. *If I want the whole bloody town knowing about it I'll have an exhibition in the foyer of the bloody Shire Hall.* And so the people of the town came to understand that Kelpie Crush would, at some time in the future, make an exhibition of his collection for them.

Very early in the poker relationship, Sinclair Johnson had suggested that he write a short 'Welcome to Siddon Rock' article on Kelpie Crush, complete with photograph. The response was short and sharp. *No.* But Sinclair was not a man to take no for an answer, and wrote a few brief paragraphs on what he thought he knew about the new man in town. When he typeset the page he found that there was a space just large enough for a photograph and thought that one of the hotel would be suitable. To get a good shot of the elegant iron lace verandah Sinclair set up his camera in the station-yard opposite the pub, and as he pressed the shutter Kelpie Crush opened the door of the bar and stepped into the street.

Sinclair lay the negative in the developing fluid, expecting to have to throw the print straight in the bin because Kelpie's blur of movement would make it unusable. But when he took it out the print was perfect, with no indication that Kelpie Crush had been in the photograph at all.

As Sinclair considered the strangeness of the photograph Abe Simmons walked in to pay his poker debt. Sinclair showed him the space in the photo where Kelpie Crush should have been. *Maybe the bloke just doesn't exist and we're all seeing things*, Abe said as he counted out a small pile of coins. *But the amount he took off me last week makes me think you'd better get your camera seen to.*

Sinclair's words stayed with Abe Simmons, and he pondered over them for the rest of the day, later discussing them with Harry Best at the pub. Harry talked to him about Plato's cave, so that by closing time Abe had decided that everyone was just a reflection of something or somewhere else and nothing could be considered real.

This night – the night Macha Connor came home – Kelpie Crush unlocked the Strangers' Room. In the light from the single hanging bulb he picked up several photographs and anchored them with drawing-pins to the wooden table. He shook the contents of an envelope marked MOTHS onto a sheet of white paper. Working quickly and flicking away body parts that fell off, he placed insects on the photographs, then, when he was satisfied with the effect, pinned them to the back of the door, in a pattern with others there.

Kelpie stood looking at the display on the door for a moment. He moved a photo or two, straightening them almost tenderly where they had skewed. Then he chose a recipe book from the pile on the table and leafed through it. He took the book and left the Strangers' Room, locking the door behind him.

In the bar, Kelpie saw a strange, throbbing light playing across the frosted windows, filling the room with shifting shadows that made it seem larger. At the window a woman was peering in, holding her hands at the side of her face, trying to see through the writing on the pane. He smiled to himself and walked to the door, but by the time he had unlocked it the woman was well down the street, passing the Farmers' Co-op.

Kelpie waited a moment before he started to follow her, alert to her every move and keeping close to shop windows, stopping now and then in case she turned around. He thought the woman was a stranger to the town and this intrigued him, as did the rhythmic waves of light and shadow that filled the street. He found himself walking faster to reach their source, which appeared to be about halfway along Wickton Street. The woman stopped in front of Meakins' Haberdashery and Ladies & Men's Apparel, and Kelpie also stopped, turning to look in the window of the Farmers' Co-op. There, instead of the usual piles of farm implements, sheep dip and drenches, worming tablets and chemicals, was the stuff of his desire.

It is to be noted that Kelpie Crush slept little, and many things occupied him during the night. In the darkest hours he would think about the boy scouts cub pack and the collection in the Strangers' Room, but it was French cuisine – or, to be more precise, reproducing French recipes as closely as possible to the original, considering the general lack of ingredients available – that kept him in the kitchen of the hotel often until daybreak. Now, here in the window of the Farmers' Co-op of Siddon Rock, here was the real thing, the ridgy-didge, the real McCoy: an authentic French market stacked to the ceiling with all that was needed to produce the *vol au vents* and *terrines*, *crêpes* and *galettes*, *quiches*, *cassoulets* and *tartes* of the recipe book he still held in his hand. And there, right at the front, was a large *casserole* of Kelpie's favourite – *blanquette de veau*. This looked quite unlike the *blanquette* he made for himself, but he could tell what it was because of the ingredients arranged around the pot. On one side of the *casserole* were stacks of the raw produce that went into its making – tiny white mushrooms, pearly baby onions, carrots and leeks tied together in graceful bunches, and, of course, perfectly trimmed and equally sized pieces of tender pink veal. On the opposite side were a jug of cream and pats of butter; a bottle of wine leaned on its side against the *casserole*, with a shining yellow lemon, surrounded by posies of herbs, at its base.

Kelpie excitedly leafed through the recipe book that he still held, quickly comparing listed ingredients with those on display. He tried to open the door of the Co-op but it was locked tight and barred. He shook the door in frustration, the light flashed and twirled around him, reflected in a row of upended saucepans that lined the front of the scene in the window. A young boy entered and began taking things from the display. *No*, Kelpie shouted, banging the recipe book on the glass. *No. Wait for me.*

The young boy seemed not to hear for a moment, then he looked up and a smile – was it of recognition? – crinkled his face.

As the light slowed to a lazy undulation Kelpie Crush watched the boy take the objects of his desires away, until all that was left in the window was the row of saucepans. Kelpie waited for the boy to come back, but he did not appear. Kelpie knelt on the pavement to look at the pans, and there was no reflection of him in the mirror-like steel that made their sides, and then they too disappeared.

Kelpie, with no thought to the woman he had been following, turned away from the window and went back to the pub. There he locked himself in the Strangers' Room, not emerging until Bluey Redall called him the next morning, wanting the keys to the bar so he could open for business.

The dust that inundated the town later that same night did not start in the usual way by appearing at the edge of the horizon as a reddish-grey smudge rushing on the town to take it in the white heat of desire. This was not a storm that lifted the earth and filled the landscape with a dull roaring and the houses with the topsoil from the paddocks. Nor was it one that began in small gasps which blew the stack of newsprint at the back door of Sinclair Johnson's printery, lifting one or two pages slightly then letting them fall, and with the next breath rattling the weathercock on the top of the Railway and Traveller's Hotel making it oscillate wildly with no true direction. No, it was not like that.

This is how it happened.

By midnight the power from the storage batteries had been drained, leaving the white light of a waning moon hanging low in the western sky as the only light in the town. One o'clock on the night Macha Connor came home was crystal-clear with a chilly wind from the south. There began, around about that time, a subtle rustling and shuffling as bush creatures became restless and, responding to a strangeness in the air, moved away from the town borders. Cockatoos and parrots with their daytime eyes flew awkwardly. Domestic pets joined them, and Maureen Mather stirred in uneasy sleep when the budgerigar flew uselessly against the bars of its cage, wanting to join the flight.

From their safe distance the animals watched when, at two o'clock, the wind stopped and the first dust rose gently from the gravelled station-yard and hovered two or three inches above the ground. At the same time, behind the Town Hall and Shire Offices, a puff or two lifted from the treeless yard.

Three minutes to three saw Young George Aberline's paddock, the one that bordered the edge of the town, begin to lift: dust wafted upwards as if from a lightly shaken blanket, rising and settling again, each time gaining more volume.

At the window of the Methodist manse, the Reverend Siegfried Butow watched the dust billow and settle. *This country*, he thought. *This appalling place.*

Siggy Butow, in a burst of existential despair at the drabness of life in war-torn England, had left the hills and dales of

Yorkshire for the new horizons of Australia. Of the dioceses that were available when he enquired, he chose this one of Siddon Rock because he felt most at home in the country: an open-air environment where he could continue his life of preaching and walking the countryside. He packed three favourite walking sticks, sturdy crooks carved from oak that he expected to help him over the hills of his new landscape.

Not for a second did he think, as he climbed the rock that first time, that he would look out to infinity and experience a gut-churning nausea that would return to him whenever he thought of that moment. Nothing in his confined experience had given him the imagination to picture the endlessness of the plains that were green for only a moment each year, nor the overwhelming vastness of the sky that held down the earth in an immense blue dome. This was not at all like his home in Yorkshire where he had written sermons in his head as he roamed green hills. This terrain was engulfing, all-encompassing, life-taking. It had no reason to be kind.

So Siggy Butow stayed within the safety of the manse next to the Methodist church. He ordered supplies by telephone for delivery from the Farmers' Co-op. Only occasionally did he venture as far as the tiny library at the Council Offices, and not at all to small settlements at the outer edges of the diocese, although he was expected to service these with the word of God. And so the nausea was joined by guilt, which resulted in insomnia.

This night Siggy was reading one of the many books he received by mail order from a large bookshop in the capital. He had become interested in archaeology and natural history since arriving in Siddon Rock, spurred by the arcane countryside that confined him to the inner streets of the town.

Now Siggy was not, nor ever had been, an advocate of Darwinism. He well understood what happened when the biblical teachings were departed from: the confusions of soul and questioning of scripture. This he would never do. Siggy understood the Bible as absolute truth organised into easy-to-understand parables for the less educated. However, tonight, when the rest of the town was well asleep and Siggy's own vital energy low, somehow an essay on the life and times of the dinosaurs had crept into his reading and seductively lured him into its text. *Just think*, he read, *how nothing ever disappears completely. While the bones of the dinosaurs became embedded in the earth, and a few of these have been recovered to tell us about them – their size and shape, and by the teeth what they ate – what about the rest? These bones presumably lay on top of the ground, in areas that were relatively stable and not subjected to the upheavals of mountains being made and seas moving together to form the large oceans. Over time the enormous heat and winds dried them to dust, and they became as one with the earth – dust to dust. Realise, too, that dust never disappears; it is with us always. So all the generations of humankind to this day have breathed in minute fragments of the dinosaur; and as an aside to this, also of the stardust thrown into earth's atmosphere by the burning-up of meteors. One could say that through our very breath we are connected with infinity.*

Siggy Butow slammed shut the book. He sat for a moment, perturbed at the idea put forward – that he, Siegfried Butow, man of God, was swallowing pieces of ancient beasts and, indeed, of ancient stars, and that this was his connection with infinity. It was a concept utterly at odds with his belief in the Bible as law.

Siggy turned to the large King James Bible that lay on a table near his armchair, opening it to Genesis. There, in chapter three, verse nineteen, he read the words he had so often said as a comfort to mourners at a graveside. Indeed, said so often that they had become rote and without meaning to him. As he read he realised he had forgotten that they were, in the first instance, words from God to Adam and Eve, a chastisement to the man and woman for giving way to temptation – *till thou return to the ground; for out of it wast thou taken: for dust thou art, and unto dust shalt thou return*. In the quiet of the night the idea seemed simple and clear. Everything came from dust; everything returned to dust. But it was as punishment for being human – there had been no dinosaurs, no dust from the stars. The Word was God.

At three minutes to three Siggy turned off the light by his armchair and walked to the window, expecting to see calm moonlight on the rooftops of Siddon Rock. He rather liked that he was probably the only person in the town to see how the tall wheat silo threw a long shadow when the setting moon was full: a darkened finger that covered

90

Wickton Street. This night, however, when he raised the blind the moonlight was a strange brownish colour and the surface of the earth rose and fell in a gentle rhythm. He pushed up the window to see better and realised that it was dust puffing from the ground, and with each rise the fall was less, as if the dust was gathering strength to take over the town. Siggy watched in mesmerised horror as the dust cloud grew until it filled the street outside the manse, thickening so that the setting moon was hidden and he could not see the church next door. His tired mind saw tiny dinosaurs riding the dust motes as they floated towards him, and he slammed shut and locked the window.

This country, he thought. *This appalling place.* He pulled the blind and went to bed, to spend a restless hour or two in a half-doze that was populated with exploding stars and thundering herds of unimaginable beasts.

By daybreak the dust had gone, although people knew there had been a dust-storm by the grittiness in the air. At the Two Mile, Brigid Connor commented to Granna, *It usually blows a bloody gale. And there's no dust in the house. It's usually covered, isn't it. A real mess. So why not this time?* Granna didn't bother to answer.

In town, those who had a cat or a dog wondered where they were, but weren't too concerned; and over the day they came home, enticed by the memory of easy food. The cockatoos stayed away for several days before they returned to the pepper tree roost.

CHAPTER FOUR

WOMEN'S BUSINESS

It could be said, I suppose, that the affairs of women are tied to the affairs of men; and that we more often than not fall into things than plan them. It's a well-known fact, though, that country women can do anything.

ELIZA MAY WINTON found herself well occupied with management of the farm at the Two Mile, as the business of Geo. Aberline Stock and Station Agent took up more and more of George's time. That she had given birth to four children in four years made her most grateful for the presence of Granna, who seemed to know exactly what was needed at any particular moment, be it during a birthing, on the farm, or with the children. Eliza's gratitude strengthened after the demise of George, which happened like this.

George, on his return from the desert, had gone from strength to strength. The sale of the houses, and renting out of the drays that carried them from the interior, gave him the finance to start a stock and station agency. He managed this alone, as he was loathe to waste money on an employee, more often than not leaving Eliza May to deal with matters at the Two Mile, with the assistance of a farmhand and Granna.

Sometimes at night, when his thoughts settled ready for sleep, a calm came over him that was similar, he thought, to the quiet place where the bush thinned and melted into desert. He remembered the chill and tang of the salt ponds he had seen on his return journey, and tried to fathom how they had come about, as they most decidedly were not there on his outward ride. Most of all he recalled the vision that had spurred him to make a decision to change his life. This invariably led to the story of his father Henry Aberline and his vision of a butterfly that was never proved to exist. *At least he tried*, George would think. *You've got to give him that.*

Only occasionally did he think that Lazarus Beatty would one day come for payment. Over the years this became less and less frequent, until the memory of the purchase was only a line in the ledger of the business, and George considered that the debt no longer existed.

At midday, on the day Lazarus Beatty walked out of the shimmering heat haze that hung over the inland and into George's office, there weren't many people around. The newly built Farmers' Co-op had only two shop assistants, and closed for lunch, and the postmaster was eating his sandwich in the telegraph booth, showering crumbs and flecks of cold lamb over the morse code key. So the eye-witness stories were from the drinkers in the pub. Now stories are like people; they change shape as they get older. Some get thinner with less detail, others pad out like the most comfortable grandmother. It's only someone who saw what happened who could see the bones of it under the padding, and Granna wasn't saying anything to anyone.

One story that was perpetuated through the Hinks family, and so sworn to by Martha Hinks as the true story, has it that Lazarus Beatty – although they didn't know his name of course – was dressed in black from head to toe, with a broad-brimmed hat pulled low over his face, so that his features were not distinguishable. *And my grandfather told me that he rode into town on a huge black horse*, Martha would say. *He said it was a manifestation of Beelzebub himself.*

Another story was that he had a revolver in his belt, but this was often questioned, as no-one knew exactly what a revolver looked like. Doctor Allen insisted that this gun had not been invented at the time. This always provoked discussion, as the only guns used in the district were the .22 rifle for nuisance birds or a .303 for wild dogs and kangaroos.

Yet another version said that the stranger did not ride into town at all but appeared in a puff of smoke right on the stroke of noon. *All the shops were closed for lunch*, the story goes, *and it was so hot that the dogs had gone to ground under the houses. Even the pepper trees at the railway side of the road were drooping. This stranger walks right up to the Stock and Station Agency door. How did he know where it was, eh? George Aberline always ate his lunch out the back but never bothered to lock the door. Everyone in the bar saw the man go in, but no-one saw him come out.*

When there was a challenge to this version – *All right then, who saw him go in?* – names of drifters and drinkers long gone were told.

If Granna was asked what had happened she always replied, *I don't know, and that's the truth of it.*

What actually took place in the office of Geo. Aberline Stock and Station Agent will never be known, for the following day George did not make an appearance in the town. Instead, he rode from the Two Mile as if to go as usual to his place of business next to the Farmers' Co-op, but at the crossroads went straight on to the salt lake rather than turning left to the town. Later that morning George's horse ambled up Wickton Street with George's lunch box tied neatly to the empty saddle.

The lake is always a natural starting point if someone goes missing, and it took no time at all for George's body to be untangled from the fallen ghost gum tree that held him just below the waterline. It puzzled some how this had happened, as this was at the perpetual pool which was the town swimming hole, and the one shallow place in the lake. The concentration of salt in the water was particularly strong there, making it difficult to sink and a good place for children to play. And where did that ghost gum come from? No-one recalled seeing a dead tree at the edge of the lake. But, as some still say, *If someone wants to drown, they will.*

On the window-ledge of Macha's room at the Two Mile stands a piece of amber that has a small black insect embedded in it. Macha found this when she was a child, at the back of an old cupboard in one of the sheds. Granna told her that Great-Grandmother Eliza May, who had been a Winton, brought it from the salt lake the day they found her husband drowned in the perpetual pool. *What did she do then?* the young Macha asked.

She ran the farm until the day she died, Granna said, *then your grandfather, Thomas, took it over. He comes to see you now and then. Well, he's the son of Eliza May Winton and George Henry Aberline. Just as you're the daughter of Brigid Connor and Charles Aberline.*

But how do I know that? Macha said.

You'd best be asking your mother about that. It's not my story to tell.

I ask her things, young Macha said, *but she says she's so busy she can't talk now. And when she does it's not like the mums of other kids. She doesn't tell me to be home or to do things, she just talks about those stories her mum told her. I don't understand at all. How can I be Irish when I live here? I should be called Siddon Rock-ish. Or Siddon-ish!*

And why am I called Connor and not Aberline if Mister Aberline is my father? Maybe Mum's just making this up. Maybe I just grew, like Topsy, and didn't have a father! She waved the book she had been reading. Granna took it. *Uncle Tom's Cabin,* she said. *Isn't this a bit old for you? But don't you be getting ideas, Miss Curiosity! Charlie Aberline is your father, and there's no getting away from that.*

But . . . Macha was not appeased.

It's still not for me to say, love. It's your mother's story, and for her to tell or not tell, as she wishes.

Alf Barber, Sybil's father and butcher to the town, had not been heard of since 1933 when he left with the boxing troupe that toured the country agricultural shows. Always eager and handy with his fists, Alf took up the challenge thrown out so cockily by the Aboriginal champion, and although the fight was declared a draw the boss offered him a place in the troupe. The fight was still talked about in the bar at the Railway and Traveller's Hotel, especially when the old-timers who travelled with the show each year were in town. *Do ya remember what a little bruiser Alf Barber was*, they'd say, *how he just kept at young Tommy Bristowe until the ref had to pull him off? And then he still kept punching, like he didn't know how to stop. And that kid, he was good too. Best gloves in the business. And strong! Just starting to run to fat, though. That's the problem. They start out all tough and wiry, then get slack and run to fat. Then they're gone.*

I remember having to stitch up young Bristowe after that fight, Doctor Allen said once. *Fifteen stitches in the face is no joke. Not sport, either.*

Seen worse than that, the old-timers would say. *That's nothing, on the circuit.*

He weren't so tough, Bert Truro always came back with – Bluey Redall reckoned it was like a tune played once a year – *he weren't so tough, just a little bloke with a little bloke's chip on the shoulder. Always out to prove themselves, little blokes. And Alf Barber took it out on anyone he could. Don't you remember, Bluey?*

Nah, Bluey'd say. *Way before I got back from London.*

Don't remember it at all. Don't know where Alf is now, either. Before anyone asks.

When Alf Barber took off he threw the keys of the shop to Sybil. *Beats cutting up lumps of meat for a living*, he told her as he rolled some rough clothes and a blanket into a swag. *Do what you like with the shop.*

As the trucks of sideshow alley left town Sybil opened the front and back doors of the butcher's shop to let fresh air flow through, and lit a fire under the old copper in the yard behind the shop. For three days she bucketed water from the shop tap to the copper, then scrubbed with hot water and lye soap which stripped layers of skin from her hands as it dissolved years of grime and accumulated meat fat from the shop walls and chopping blocks. She pulled out the broken fly screens from the display window, and from the Farmers' Co-op bought netting and timber which she made into new screens by copying the construction of the old ones. She turned away offers of help. *I'll do it myself*, she said. *Then I don't owe no-one.*

She's just a girl, the town said, *How can she know anything about butchering?* forgetting that Sybil had been in the shop with her father since she was knee-high to a grasshopper. *How can a woman kill beasts? How can she be strong enough to carry the carcasses? How can she find the money to do all this?* No-one saw her slip into the manager's residence at the rear of the State and Farmers' Bank one night, but she was well noticed in the bank the next day when she arrived for her appointment with the manager to arrange a loan for the business.

The day after Macha came home, and twelve years after Alf Barber left town, Sybil hired Jack Mulligan and his brother Jimmy to bring their tractors into town. *Come tomorrow morning*, she said. *Bring a clearing chain at least fifty yards long.* And so at six o'clock on a still winter's morning – *and on a Sunday, too*, the town whispered, when the story was told and re-told – the Mulligan brothers slung a chain around the dilapidated shack where Alf Barber had lived, and slowly pulled it forward into a tumbled heap of sticks and tin.

Drawn by the roar of tractors in the streets, people stood in the gravelled road watching the demolition. They saw remnants of the Barbers' domestic life – the bent iron of a bedstead, an unbroken porcelain chamber-pot with improbably pink roses twined among bright green leaves, several flattened saucepans, some tin plates, and other battered utensils whose uses were difficult to identify. A wardrobe with its door swinging from one hinge leaned against the remains of the fireplace, the cracked mirror reflecting crazy angles of broken timber, townspeople and sky as its momentum slowly worked the remaining hinge out of the cabinet. As the door fell it revealed to the town Alf Barber's two pairs of trousers and three shirts still hanging from the rod, and a tumble of blue-and-white-striped aprons on the floor of the wardrobe.

Jack Mulligan made to switch off the engine of his tractor but Sybil waved toward the back fence where the outdoor lavatory still stood, and shouted above the engine noise that the rubble should be pulled into a tighter heap.

On the second pass of the chain the cracked boards of the lavatory disintegrated into the pile, as did the wooden seat and toilet can it contained. The onlookers, not expecting any smell from the old can after so many years, gasped and moved back with hands held to mouth and nose as a foul miasma rose. Alistair Meakins – ever one for taking care of a sensitive nose and stomach – retched violently and left the scene, giving in to the sudden urge for a pot of tea in the calm of his own back verandah.

Brigid Connor covered her nose and commented to Granna that it was just as well a ghost's sense of smell wasn't good, as the stench of Alf Barber was like nothing she'd ever smelt before. *Can't smell a thing*, Granna said cheerfully. Maureen Mather, in her bed at the other side of town, struggled into her wheelchair and tried to close the windows against the sudden gust of malodorous wind. Even Kelpie Crush paled slightly, and found that using shallow, panting breaths made the odour a little more bearable. Kelpie, though, was more drawn forward than pushed back, wanting in a vague sort of way to find the source of the corruption.

Sybil directed the tractors into the street and well away from the rubble. In the silence after the roaring engines were turned off the bells from the Catholic church were suddenly loud, but no-one spoke and no-one moved. The play was not finished yet. Sybil picked up a bucket and threw kerosene over the pile, splashing it around well. She crouched down and from her pocket took a packet of matches, struck one and touched it to a piece of saturated wood.

Two minutes, they say in the telling, *two minutes and that old shack went up like a beacon. Old wood it was. Mainly deal and pine from those packing cases the Farmers' Co-op used to get machine parts in. And one room was made from the big container that Ford sedan arrived in for old Thomas Aberline.*

Flames followed the rivulets of kerosene into the heart of the pile and at first there was a smokeless blaze. Then the fire found Alf Barber's shit, dried and refined to a fine fuel by time, and a ball of purple and orange smoke burst into the sky and spread across the town, dropping black ashes on the exposed heads of those watching. Upwards and outwards it spread, the sudden wind catching the ash and residue.

Sybil retreated from the flames and looked at the people standing in the street. *A good barbecue now,* she said. *But this was Alf Barber's house, and you knew what he was doing in it. All of you knew, and not one of you tried to stop him.* And Sybil Barber left the ashes of her father's house for her own home near the salt lake.

On the evening of the day Alf Barber went off with the boxing troupe those twelve years ago, Sybil had walked out to the lake whose surface glinted icily in the setting sun. At the edge stood eucalypts petrified by the salt water into stark grey sculptures: ghosts of trees past reflecting in the surface of the salt lake. *I wonder how long the lake has been here,* she thought, but no-one in the town could have answered this had she asked; as far as the town remembered, the lake had always been there.

Sybil also saw that the salt had crept across the ground and closer to the road since she had been here the summer before, and was climbing the wooden posts of Brigid Connor's boundary fence. Sybil went to tell Brigid about the fence, and at the same time she asked if she could lease a small tract of land near the salt lake, to build a house for herself. *That piece of land's no bloody use to man or beast with the friggin' salt encroachment*, Brigid said. *It's not worth anything to me, so why don't you just use a bit wherever you want.*

Sybil chose a small rise that was hardly discernible to the eye to site her house, which was small and round with doors opening to the pale soil patched with crystals of white. *It's round*, she told anyone who asked, *so that I can see the whole world around me and no-one can catch me by surprise.* Walls were built of sun-dried bricks made from a small clay-pan between the lake and the piece of bush known as the Yackoo. She made these herself with the help of the lovers who repaid her with a day's work.

Rather like a large mushroom, Young George Aberline commented as the roof of Sybil's new home took shape. There it sat above the shortened tower that was the bulk of the house. Its extension was as wide as a verandah and protected the windows from the rain and all but the very low sun. From here Sybil, looking north-west, could see over the lake to farms on the other side. To the north she looked across paddocks and small patches of remaining bush, and when she turned eastwards she saw the thick bush of the Yackoo. The town was hidden by the rock, and this was how she liked it.

When Macha began to regularly patrol the borders of the town to keep it safe at night, she found that Sybil's house was too isolated to include in the circuit. It was, however, on the route to the Yackoo or to Nell's hut, and each time she walked these paths Macha checked the house, whether Sybil was home or working at the shop. Sybil found that having Macha Connor peer in the windows and check the doors was actually a comforting thing, and she never objected.

It was a strange thing with Nell – the people of the town knew her name and knew she worked at the hospital or cleaned the school, because this was when her name would come into the conversation. But ask anyone to say when they last saw Nell, or to describe what she looked like, and there'd be clicking of tongues, thoughtful expressions and, eventually, an admission of *Well, can't say really,* or *Don't quite remember.*

Harry Best the headmaster knew her, of course, because she cleaned the school; as did Bert Truro the hospital orderly and town grave-digger; and, of course, the matron of the hospital. But generally she was an unseen name. Even when she sat with her dingoes on the steps of the war memorial at night she was invisible. There were complaints to the Council on several occasions about the dingoes coming into the main street of the town, mutterings of *What about the children?* or *Bloody things are spooky, they just sit there and watch ya.* Inevitably, someone from the Council would be dispatched to do something about it, and just as inevitably the dogs would disappear for a while. But as sure as the sun rises and sets they'd be back. Yet no-one saw Nell there, talking to her dogs and keeping them quietly at her side.

Nell made sure the dingoes stayed at her hut when she went to the hospital where she was employed, under sufferance, by Matron Sullivan. Matron knew that she could not find anyone except Nell to spend as much time cleaning and cooking for such a mean wage.

Matron Sullivan, as she regularly told the Hospital Board of Directors, *tried to instil some idea of time into this person*, but to no avail: Nell arrived and left seemingly at will. Matron even went to the lengths of giving Nell an old alarm clock from her own store of things, but this charitable act did not achieve Nell's arrival at the same time each day, and Matron told the Board that Nell was too stupid to understand time. It was just as well, then, that Matron did not see Nell throw the clock into the salt lake.

Matron Sullivan was an onlooker at the clearing of Alf Barber's house. On the way back to the hospital she talked at Bert Truro, who walked with her. *What could be so bad,* she said, *as to make someone so vengeful?* She conjectured about such a hate as she mounted the steps of the hospital verandah, and did not see Nell washing the floorboards with long, slow strokes. Matron Sullivan tumbled, spilling water and profanities over Nell and across the verandah. Nell tried to close her ears but from the bucket sloshed a river of insults and arrogance that adhered to her skin like un-rinsed soap, clogging her pores so that she could not breathe.

Bert Truro, bending to help Matron from the floor, glanced up to see what Nell was doing, and was surprised to see a woman he didn't know, a woman bigger and more angular than the rounded softness of Nell. He decided, when thinking about this later, that it was a trick of angle and light, as it was definitely Nell who spoke soft words of apology and helped him carry Matron Sullivan to a bed in the women's ward.

The sprain to Matron Sullivan's foot was slight, in keeping with the gentle fall over the bucket of dirty water, but she was laid up for several days. Nell, in an effort to cheer her, prepared the hearty soups and stews that she knew Matron liked so well. However, Matron Sullivan became angrier and more agitated after each meal, snapping at Nell about over-cooked meat and under-cooked vegetables; about the thickness of the gravy and the thinness of the custard on the steamed pudding. She even complained about the slipperiness and hardness of the starched sheets – a condition for which she blamed Nell, although it had been Matron herself who specified that bed linen was to be starched. And after each meal and each complaint Nell felt her skin become more clogged and her breathing more laboured.

On the morning of the fourth day, Nell lightly boiled two eggs and toasted the white bread that Matron said made the best toast. She prepared a breakfast tray by covering an ordinary ward tray with a small embroidered cloth and matching serviette. On this she placed two small plates from the set usually kept for official lunches and a silver teaspoon for the eggs. She added a pot of tea and a cup with a little milk in it, covered the tray with another white cloth and carried it down the long passageway to the women's ward. There she placed it on the bedside table, as Matron was still asleep, and left quietly, thinking she should not wake her.

Some time later there was a mighty clatter and bang from the ward. Bert Truro dropped the bundle of wood he was bringing in for the kitchen fire and ran down the corridor to the ward, closely followed by Nell. There they found the breakfast tray overturned on the floor and an angry Matron Sullivan struggling off the bed. Bert bent to pick up the tray, but Matron stopped him. *Let that black bitch do it*, she shouted, and even the stolid Bert winced back from the spray of venom. *Make that stupid black bitch clean it up. She made the mess. She fixes it.*

Bert helped Matron Sullivan to a chair on the side verandah, where he propped her foot on a stool. *I'm staying here until that bed linen is washed and the bed remade with the same sheets*, she said. *And it'd better be soon.*

Nell picked up the tray and the mess of broken china, egg and tea. Her skin itched with the poison hanging in the air; she could feel the surface flaking away, and wondered how much of herself she could lose before disappearing entirely. She fetched hot water and a rag and wiped the bedside table and the floor. Then she took the soiled sheets from the bed and went to the laundry where hot water was already bubbling in the copper, ready for the day's normal laundry.

Nell shook shaved soap into the boiling water and threw in the sheets from Matron Sullivan's bed, pushing them under the suds with a stick. After a few minutes she heaved them out into a large cement trough of cold water. Her skin still itched, the rough scaliness had become worse, and now her chest was heavy with the effort to breathe. Nell plunged her arms into the trough with the sheets, kneading them under the water to get rid of the soap. As she did a sulphurous-looking sludge rose to the surface, and she wondered what it was. She took her hands from the suds to run a second trough of water for rinsing, and realised that the skin on her arms had stopped itching and had smoothed to a soft sheen.

Nell looked at the water in the trough where the sheets were, at the jaundiced scum lying like algae on the surface, and a small hum started in the back of her throat. She shut the door to the laundry and peeled off her apron and then her dress and climbed into the water with the sheets. As Nell lowered herself into the water it seethed as if with a million tiny fish, as the poison from Matron Sullivan washed from Nell's skin. Nell pulled the sheets around her, wrapping them as tightly as she could as she sat in the washing trough.

When Nell climbed out she felt light and cool: her skin was fresh and clear and she breathed deeply. The water in the trough was darkly yellow, but the sheets rose white to the surface, the colour not marking them.

Nell hummed as she dressed, and hummed louder as she pulled the dripping sheets from the trough, ignoring the wringer attached to the trough which would normally squeeze out excess water. She staggered slightly under the weight of the sheets as she carried them to the clothesline, where she pegged them in a single layer so they would dry quickly.

When the sheets were dry Nell folded them and took them to the ward, swiftly making up Matron Sullivan's bed. *No starch*, she said to Matron through the French doors that opened onto the verandah. *Now they're soft for you.* Then she helped Matron from the chair into the bed.

On the evening of that day Doctor Allen looked in to see how Matron was faring. He could not understand why she had a fever. *It's only a sprain*, he said. *Nothing at all, really. And certainly no reason for a fever like this.* But in Matron Sullivan's body unknown organisms altered the symmetry, making her temperature rise and fever rage.

Doctor Allen's main concern, though, was to find what was making Matron's skin flake and peel away in thick strips as she scratched desperately, trying to relieve the deep and painful itch that would not be eased by any panacea from the hospital pharmacy. He consulted medical texts and telephoned every expert he knew, trying to find a precedent. He checked diseases that started in the soil and in the air, and wondered if he was going to have an epidemic of something caused by the miasma released from Alf Barber's dunny. In short, he did all that was humanly possible for Matron Sullivan, but the fever was too fast and the itch too deeply embedded under the skin to relieve, and two days later on the death certificate he wrote *Unknown fever. Unknown etiogenic agent.*

As a child Macha Connor was fascinated by the cloud of tiny blue shapes that accompanied Marge Redall wherever she went, sometimes swarming around her head like a large blue hat, at other times drifting languidly along behind her as a gracious blue veil. She asked Granna what it was and where she, Macha, could get one. *It's not for you to have, Mach*, Granna said with a hug. *We all carry things with us that no-one else can have. You'll have your own, when you get older. You'll just have to wait until then.*

Will they be blue like Marge's? Macha asked.

No love, Granna said. *They'll be inside you, where no-one else can see.*

But what if I want other people to see. Like Marge's blue cloud?

Marge doesn't really want them out there to be seen. She didn't have any choice. But you, my sweet, you won't talk about yours at all. Not to anyone.

But you say I talk too much anyway. Macha laughed. *And Mum's always telling me to be quiet. So maybe then you'll both be happy.*

We're always happy with you around, Granna said.
We always will be.

To the people of Siddon Rock, the farmers of the district,
and the various travelling salesmen who stayed overnight
at the Railway and Traveller's Hotel, Marge Redall was the
stereotypical publican's wife. Large, loud and brash, she
looked after the bar when an extra hand was needed and
made sure the kitchen produced good, filling and basic
food. *These blokes don't want anything fancy,* she'd said to
Bluey when they first took over from his father. *As long as
there's a lot of it, they'll be happy.* And happy they were, the
pub known for its generous plates of food, well-pulled beer,
and easy welcome from Bluey and Marge.

Marge's swarm of tiny blue shapes had arrived with
her when Bluey Redall brought her back from Europe.
When people got around to asking her what they were she
just said, *a nuisance,* and it was left at that.

While she was loathe to discuss herself with other
people, Marge Redall recalled vividly when she was six
years old and sat for the first time at the piano. Mrs Enright
opened *Teaching Little Fingers to Play.* There on the page in
front of Marjorie were black shapes that Mrs Enright said
made music.

That's not music, Marjorie said.

Luckily for Marjorie, Mrs Enright had been around
music and musicians for more years than she cared to recall,
and was wise enough to take the child away from the piano

and ask her to show her what music was. So Marjorie told her about the sounds that were with her all the time. She hummed and danced the rhythms of her life, from waves breaking on the beach near her home to the clangity-clang of city trams. The pop-pop of her father's car was there, as was a sliding note that Mrs Enright thought to be from the opera *Turandot*.

Mrs Enright listened and watched. Then she said, *Your music is just for you, Marjorie, and no-one else can hear it quite like you do. But if you learn which notes go with which keys on the piano, then maybe you'll be able to copy some of it, so that you can show other people what your music is.*

And so Marjorie began the journey towards her music. We don't need to follow the beginning story too closely. It's sufficient to know that once she moved away from the piano to the more suggestive tones of the clarinet, Marjorie flew up the crescendo of a stellar musical career. But the harmonies of Beethoven and Bach, and even the soaring genius of Mozart, had no place for the wild music that Marjorie still carried with her.

So there Marjorie was, at what appeared to be an impasse in her life, in that late summer of 1935. She had just left the London Symphony and was about to leave for Berlin, enticed by the idea of being part of a new ensemble.

On her last night in London her bags were packed and she was ready to go. The taxi was ordered for early the next morning. But there was a touch of chill in the night air, and in the yellowish glow from street lights the first dying leaves from beech and oak trees spun to the ground.

Was it excitement at the new venture, or a touch of fear about going to a strange country from where came whisperings of war, that kept Marjorie awake and drew her into the streets of Soho so late at night? She was walking slowly along, looking into shop windows and obviously reluctant to go back to her packed-up flat.

Someone opened the door at the bottom of a set of steps leading to a basement, and music flowed out. *Is this a private party?* she asked the man who came up the steps. *You can go in, lady,* he said. *Anyone can go in.*

She enjoyed the music; it was modern, simple and boppy, different from her own classical world and easy to let slip into the background as she bought herself a drink and settled in a booth near the low platform stage. But as she did so the trio made its final flourish – it was very late, after all – and the few people in the audience left quickly.

The saxophonist started to pack up, but the piano player lit a cigarette and settled back on the piano stool, running his fingers up and down the keyboard in cadences with a slight syncopation, doodling on the black notes. The drummer touched brushes over the skins, giving *whooshy-swish* support to the doodles. The sax player looked at them and smiled. He took a long swig from a glass, wiped his lips, and joined in the improvisation.

Then the drums took over, and the notes became a slow-moving train. The piano player picked up the rhythm, and waves rolled in on a beach and then receded as the saxophone blew up a summer storm. Marjorie was surrounded by her music, *was* her music. Marjorie had found jazz.

On the table where the open saxophone case lay was another, familiarly shaped, case. Marjorie opened it, put together the pieces of the clarinet, held it up to the sax player with a question in her eyes. He nodded, and she stepped into jazz and out of the Berlin quartet. As she lifted the clarinet to her lips, her music gathered around her and she saw that it was made of deep, vibrant blue notes.

Marjorie stayed and played, forgoing Berlin, classical quartets and symphony orchestras for a hole-in-the-wall basement, jazz and the blues. She formed a casual friendship with the barman, a young Australian from a country town who was working his way around Europe.

As he cleaned the bar down early one morning, the barman mentioned that he was going home. *My dad's died,* he said. *I've gotta go back soon and look after things. D'ya want to come home?*

Marjorie was startled, surprised that he could even think she'd want to leave London and the jazz. *Whatever for?* she said. *This is my life here.*

But over the next month the seed took root, watered by the barman's daily question: *Sure ya don't want to come home?* The night he cleaned down the bar for the last time and walked out of the club into a smoggy and icy London early morning, Marjorie felt the call of the Australian sun, and walked out with him.

On the long, slow voyage across the English Channel, through the Mediterranean to the Suez Canal and down into the Indian Ocean, Marjorie and the barman watched the oceans change from cold grey through all shades of blue and green. As they saw the low, flat coastline of home he said, *You know I've gotta take over the family pub. D'ya want to come too?*

This time there was no hesitation for Marjorie, no *But what about my music?* No *What am I going to?* In fact, not a second passed before she answered.

Why not? Marjorie replied, and her blue notes settled on her shoulders with barely a sigh.

On the train, as it rocked its way across flat, pale-soiled land towards Bluey's home town, Bluey put his arm around her. *Ya going to miss all that?* he said. And Marge took it to mean, *Are you going to be happy staying here at the edge of the outback, or are you going to want to go back to Europe and the music?*

Nah, she said. *This'll be just fine. There's music everywhere.*

Bluey stood firmly on the floor of the swaying train. *Can you hear it here, Margie?* Marge nodded, feeling through the soles of her feet a sound deeper than the rhythm of the train, a sombre, more insistent note.

Marge soon found the rhythms of Siddon Rock were quieter and rougher than any she had experienced, more apparently singular, but with a supportive, interwoven complexity. It took only a short time for her to settle into the routine.

Sometimes when the telephone rang and Marge picked up the receiver there was a sea-like silence broken by a single note that blew a dark hole in her day. Most times it was a flattened fifth note, but now and then a bent third emerged. At these times Marge took herself to the top of Siddon Rock itself, until the blues she found in a basement in Soho retreated to the edge of her vision. Then she would go back to Bluey Redall and his pub.

CHAPTER FIVE
SECRET PLACES: KNOWING AND FORGETTING

There are things we know we know, things we think we know, and things we know we don't know. But the trickiest of all are the things we think we know, but really don't.

LIFE AT THE TWO MILE resumed a daily rhythm different from before Macha went to war; different, too, from those established while she was away. The silence she had left behind had been strange for Brigid and Granna, used as they were to the cheerful, noisy efficiency of Macha around the farm, but over time they had become accustomed to it. Now she was home, the silence grew deeper and darker, asking something of the two women, but even Granna could not know what this was.

Brigid would sit next to Macha as she stared from the verandah towards the salt lake with her rifle at her side. She would touch her arm and tell her the stories she had told her when she was a child, willing her words to break through the silence. Granna could see the heart-pain in Brigid, and could offer nothing to ease it.

Macha pulled her bed onto the north verandah but she did not sleep. She could not sleep. If Brigid or Granna had asked, *Why can't you sleep, Macha Machushla?*, Macha, had she replied, would have said, *Sleep is dangerous.*

When Macha was not on the verandah she was walking the paddocks or was far out on the plains. Farmers and townspeople alike quickly became used to seeing Macha around the district, clad in only army boots and hat and carrying the rifle. *If that's what she wants, that's what she can do,* Young George said, the first time he saw his niece walking across his paddocks. *I reckon that whatever she's been through's given her the right to do what she likes.* And no-one argued with him, not even once.

Will she be safe? Brigid asked Granna, who seemed not to hear the question. Brigid imagined Macha's Irish-fair skin burning in the fierce inland heat or being penetrated by poisonous wild things that lived in the bush. But the sun did not affect Macha, nor did the bitter chill of an inland winter night. And the bush to her was a place of safety.

The arrival of her kit, three weeks after she had walked into town, made Macha go to that piece of bush known as the Yackoo for the first time since she came home. There she was, gazing out to the salt lake when the station-master, Kenneth Placer, phoned Brigid Connor to tell her that a kit belonging to Corporal M. Connor had been at the station for days, and please to pick it up.

Goin' in to pick up your kit, Brigid said to Macha, and when she looked up Macha was gone, heading across the paddocks towards the Yackoo.

All her life Macha had gone into the Yackoo, not realising that it was an impenetrable place until Fatman Aberline told her. *How d'ya get through that mallee?* he asked. *Dad said it's like a brick wall.*

Macha was amazed. *I just walk in*, she said. *It's easy. Just walk in*, and she took Fatman in with her at times, until he was thirteen. Then the bush seemed to get thicker and more resistant to him. He found it too difficult to slide his new large body through the spaces between the trees, and so he stopped going.

Now, Macha still found it easy to *just walk in*. Beyond the external rim of thick scrub the interior of the Yackoo was park-like. The high, loose leaf canopy of white-trunked eucalypts was tipped with bronze new growth that fractured sunlight as it slanted down, as clear and clean as the sound of a bell.

Macha walked quietly, stealthily, through the trees, avoiding dry twigs as if she might surprise someone at rest in the park. The rifle seemed somehow unbefitting to this place.

At the centre was a lean-to made from long branches propped against a tree, their ends anchored firmly in the ground. These had cross-struts tied with wire – small beams to hold the structure firm. Part of the frame was packed with grass to give solid walls and form a partially enclosed shelter. A fragile-looking thing, this, but it had stood there since the day the twelve-year-old Macha had built it to show Fatman Aberline how it was done.

Macha leaned the rifle on the tree and took off the hat. She stretched up towards the leaf canopy of the trees, and in the dappling play of sun and shadow on her white body and pale red hair, she could have been a young tree growing towards the light. She inspected the lean-to, then settled herself in its shelter with her back against the tree. There she stayed until dusk, when she returned to the Two Mile.

The farmers whose land abutted the Yackoo's extensive edges often looked longingly at the large, almost circular area of thick mallee scrub. They could see it disappear, replaced by paddocks of wheat or sown pasture feeding stolid sheep. But their visions always came to nothing as they suddenly realised the impracticality of clearing such a dense and inhospitable place. All, that is, except Macha's uncle Young George Aberline.

Just before the war Young George tried to clear the Yackoo, as had his father Thomas before him. The town had watched with interest as he scorned the old and weak equipment of the Mulligan brothers and brought in Berthold's Bush Bashers, a contracting company that specialised in broad-acre clearing.

The noise started when the Bashers' equipment trundled through town: bulldozers the size of mountains; tractors that snorted and roared like the bunyip in stories told to fractious kids; chains as thick and solid as Fatman Aberline's thigh. Children – who, like animals, know of the unusual before it happens – heard the cavalcade well before it reached the town and rushed from the classroom. They hung on the school fence, overawed by the bright orange monsters unlike anything they'd ever seen.

That night in the pub the Bashers team talked figures, numbers, statistics. They told the locals just how good these machines were: *Nothing like 'em anywhere in Australia*, they said. *Boss had them specially imported from America. They do things big over there, ya know.*

The young blokes were excited, saying things like, *It's about bloody time someone used that land. Bloody waste otherwise, that's what it is.* The old-timers held their tongues, knowing what they knew. They stayed silent when the largest bulldozer blew its engine as it pushed towards the first line of bush. The explosion ripped apart the somnolent morning as a great ball of fire billowed against the calm blue of the sky. The flames lit the town with a garish yellow light and the outline of the Yackoo shimmered like a mirage through the burning fumes.

Not a word was said as the thick chains broke against small trees or were flung into the air by the whippy trunks of mallee. They snapped back hungrily towards the Bashers crew and thumped to earth, raising a cloud of dust that coated everything in the town with a layer of pale grit.

They held their counsel when tractor tyres blew out, penetrated by sharp branches hidden under the surface of the ground, creating the need for running repairs on site. Herbie Hinks, who owned the one small garage in town, pulled his son from school and set him to running the petrol pump for the townspeople, leaving Herbie free to look after the Bashers' tyres and repairs. *Making a mint*, he said. *Don't matter if he misses a couple of readin' lessons.*

In the pub after another frustrating day, the contractors muttered things like: *Never seen such a bloody impossible piece of land* and *This bush is fuckin' up everything that goes near it.* Young George insisted they keep trying. He had inherited the firm will – some would say stubbornness – of his grandmother, Eliza May Winton, and didn't like to be beaten. *Payin' ya good money to do this*, he said. *Ya gotta give it a decent go.*

One morning, after a particularly bad day that had seen all the Bashers' bulldozers stopped by one thing or another, there was no roar of engines to wake the town at daybreak. Herbie Hinks drove out to see what was going on, and came back amazed. *Not a bloody soul in sight*, he said. *All that machinery's just sitting there in Young George's paddock, and there's no-one around.*

And no-one from Berthold's Bush Bashers was ever there again. They left the monolithic pieces of machinery standing in a row facing the Yackoo, looking for all the world like huge creatures waiting for a chance to enter. There they stayed, a memorial to the battle between man and the bush. Over the years, salt blown from the lake rusted them to surreal shapes that seemed to have always been a part of the landscape.

Sue us if you want, the manager of Berthold's Bush Bashers said to Young George when he telephoned him to see what was happening. *Won't do you no good. After this we're broke anyways.*

That night Young George stayed at the bar until his son David and Fatman Aberline tied him onto the back of his truck and drove him home. *Should a body meet a body*, Young George sang through the shake and rattle as the truck bounced down the track to his farm, *comin' thru the rye/Should a body mow a body/need a body cry?*

Fatman Aberline was riding his motorbike slowly alongside the truck and talking through the window to his cousin. He laughed when he heard Young George's song. *Y'know what our grandad Tom said, after he tried to clear the Yackoo? 'That bloody piece of bush is harder to mow than a bloody woman, not letting you in when ya want to.' But silly bugger, Young George. You'd reckon he'd have learnt that the Yackoo is bad luck.*

But *bad luck* was not how the old-timers saw it. To Young George they said, *Well, you know the Yackoo, it always had a mind of its own*. But *bloody stupid* was the general opinion or *jinxed*. And old stories circulated: about how blokes would try to walk through the Yackoo and not come back; or, if they made it, how they'd be delirious for days and not recall what happened. *Remember that young fella from the goldfields?* Bluey Redall said. *I was just a kid. He went there to camp – said he wanted some trees after all the bloody sand he'd seen. Well no-one saw him again, did they!*

Then Bert Truro, who was not prone to smiling, said, *Old Nell goes there all the time. Bloody black gin practically lives there, when she's not in the creek-bed.* He blew the froth off his beer and took a long swill. *I reckon she's cursed it, so's no-one else can go there.*

Kelpie Crush, who usually contributed nothing to bar gossip, said sharply, *Curses aren't so easily laid, old man. They usually take generations to work.* But a mutter rumbled through the few men left at the bar at this late hour. *Yeah*, someone said, and the voice could have belonged to any one of them, *maybe we should just ask her about it all.* And a small group of men found themselves standing outside Nell's hut in the ancient creek-bed shouting for her to come out, although she was obviously not there. *Prob'ly in the Yackoo*, someone muttered. *I aren't goin' there.*

Bert Truro took a can of petrol from the back of his ute and started splashing it on the walls of the hut. *Goin' to get rid of the flea-ridden dump once and f'all.* Suddenly there was no-one standing with him as the others slunk off towards the town, and stumbled away home.

Bert emptied the rest of the can at the doorway and was feeling through his pockets for a match when a chorus of howls startled him. Nell strode towards him, her dingoes at heel, her anger as sharp and crackling as the flames Bert was about to light. If Bert would tell the truth, which he was indisposed to do at any time, he would say that at first he thought this woman was a stranger, for she was surely not the Nell he saw working in the kitchen at the hospital. That Nell was a small, soft woman who looked at no-one as she went about her tasks. This woman striding through the night surrounded by wild dogs was tall and powerful, with one dangerous-looking hand stretched towards him. The sight was too

much for his beery mind, and he fled to the safety of his
ute and then back to town, never to speak to anyone of
the incident.

As Macha entered the Yackoo, back at the Two Mile Brigid
had returned from the railway station. She emptied the
kit-bag onto the verandah, reeling back at the odour that
emanated from it – a smell, as Granna said, *like something
died and then died again . . . and not happy with that, died
a third time*. The stink took days to dissipate, and people
in the town asked about the exotic and repulsive smell that
wafted in from the Two Mile. Some went to the Roads Board
Office to complain, but Gawain Evans said that he had no
idea what the smell was and denied any knowledge of its
source. But then he had never been out of the town in his
life, let alone overseas.

In the bottom of the bag, covered with dirt that had a
foreign texture and colour, was a worn leather case holding
a camera, the likes of which had not been seen in Siddon
Rock. Brigid took the camera from its case and wiped
it over and over with a cloth dampened with kerosene,
removing layers of a black glue-like substance which, she
told Granna after hours of working over it, *is like nothin'
in God's kingdom and worse than the devil to get off*. When
the camera was clean they could see that it was dented and
scratched and altogether gave the appearance of being well
used. On the bottom of the camera was a name they did not
know – Leica.

The camera-case itself Granna cleaned with saddle-soap. As the grime was removed, writing was revealed engraved in the leather, but they could make neither head nor tail of the inscription: *Meinem Sohn Hansi. Halte dein Leben fest, in Liebe, Mütterchen.*

Brigid took the used film from the camera and another that was inside the case. *I'll get these developed for her*, she said. *I'll take them to Albey at the chemist's when I'm in town tomorrow.*

When Brigid collected the developed film later in the week, Albey was apologetic: *Not sure how these will be, Brig*, he said. *It's a damned interesting type of film, though. I've seen nothing like it before. You've got to hand it to those Germans, they certainly know what they're doing when it comes to this sort of thing.*

Macha was in her usual place on the verandah when Brigid called to her, *Come and look, Macha, I've got your photos here.* When Brigid looked around Macha had disappeared, and she heard her bedroom door close behind her.

Brigid opened the envelope that held prints from the roll of film in the camera case. They were all of young men in the uniform of the German army. *So young*, she said, looking at their playful poses. *Just boys, really.*

The photos from the roll of film that had been in the camera were altogether a different matter. Granna picked them up and ran her thumb down the edge of the pile, making them flick into motion. She went silent, and flicked again. Then again. *Oh no*, she said. *Oh no.* She started towards the kitchen fireplace, but Brigid grasped her arm.

What is it? You can't burn them. They're Macha's. Let me see.

You shouldn't, Granna said. *Brig, you really shouldn't.*

But Brigid Connor took the pile of photos and mimicked Granna's flicking motion, so that the images ran into movement. She did it again, then looked at Granna. *What does this mean?*

The first flickering images showed women with arms around their children – no men were there – standing in a row against the wall of a wooden church. Soldiers stood with guns trained on the group, and a photographer was at one side recording the scene. A German officer walked up and down in front of the women. The words shouted were in the aggressive thrust of his head. *Where are they; tell me now.* But no-one spoke; no-one moved. The man pulled a child from the row and pushed her onto her knees in the dust, his pistol at her head. *Where are they; tell me now.* Then the child was lying in the dirt, her head in a dark stain on the ground.

Brigid dropped the photos onto the table. *Who took these? Granna, where was our Macha? How did she get these?*

Granna picked up the photos again, and Brigid looked over her shoulder. Now the church was burning fiercely, and the street was empty except for the dead child and the soldiers lying back resting, and one who stood with a machine-gun trained on the door of the church.

Who could watch such horror, Brigid said. *Who could stand there and take such photos.* Then things changed.

Something had made the photographer walk away from the village. An unusual sound from the forest, maybe? Now the scene was of trees, and there, up a large tree close to the photographer, was a shadowy shape pale against the blackness of the forest.

If I didn't know better, I'd swear that's Macha, Brigid said. *But it's a bloke. Infantry by the look of it. Definitely an Australian uniform. But Mach was a nurse, so it can't be her.*

Granna's hands shook as she went to the window where the light was brighter. As she held the photographs up, the better to see them, they twisted and the angle of vision altered. Now the women saw, as if high above a tableau, the photographer walking away from the village into the edge of the forest, and aiming the camera all around him. They saw him drop the camera and raise his arms in the classical gesture of surrender; and then he was on the ground with the Australian standing over him.

Granna scooped up the photos and threw them into the kitchen fire.

But that was Macha, wasn't it. How ever did she get there? And in the infantry? And she would have seen . . . Brigid broke off, hardly able to speak, and for a moment she touched her daughter's mind. *She would have seen that horror. Oh God. The horror.*

Brigid and Granna heard the bang of the cupboard

on the verandah where the bedrolls were kept, the *click-thunk* of a rifle bolt being checked, and then the thud of Macha's boots as she walked across the hard earth of the house-yard. Brigid started to move towards the door but Granna put a hand on her arm. *Best let her be, Brig. She'll go to the Yackoo. It's a safe place for her.*

We should've thrown out that bloody Hun camera and the bloody film, Brigid said. *Mind our own friggin' business, is what we should've done. Now she won't come home for who knows how long.*

And this is indeed what happened. Macha went back to her shelter at the centre of the Yackoo, where she lit a small fire in a circle of stones and kept it alight with twigs and broken-up pieces of dead wood. There she sat with the rifle and the camera by her side in the twitching, sighing bush until night. Then she wrapped the camera in a blanket from the bedroll and put it under a pile of leaves in the corner of the shelter, checked her rifle, and marched out of the bush towards the town of Siddon Rock.

Macha's change from army nurse to infantryman came about as things often do: with no fuss or bother, no grand plots or plans, but as the result of propitious circumstance.

It was by chance that Macha was the only specialist nurse available on the night Corporal Mark Connor was admitted to the isolation tent. When Mark was occasionally conscious during the long days and longer nights, they talked about their name similarity, and of how their long, thin bodies, red hair and freckled, pale complexions must surely be a trait of the Connor clan from way back. *I always wanted the other Irish look*, Macha said. *You know, the black hair and blue eyes.*

Ah, me too, Mark said through his pain. *But my mother told me I was of the line of Cuchulain and had to put up with his colouring if I wanted his courage.*

Mine too, said Macha, as she re-dressed his wounds yet again. *Mine too.*

As the days passed, Mark faded and Macha could see the layers of his body. At first there was a translucence of the skin which slid away from the freckles burned deep into his face and hands by the hot sun of his childhood. Flesh became mist and drifted off, leaving a broken skeleton and damaged internal organs lying in bas-relief against the rough field-hospital bedding, until they too became as misty and inexact as a photogram image.

Mark disappeared completely at three o'clock one morning – the hour of the wolf when the spirit is at its lowest ebb. It seemed to Macha entirely natural to put on his uniform, pick up his pack and rifle and walk out into the landscape of war.

That Mark and Macha were no longer at the hospital went generally unremarked. Some probably assumed that he had recovered enough to be transferred and that Macha had gone with him as escort. Two nurses, rushing from the barracks tent to the general ward, said they saw him walk out towards the front, so maybe he had recovered and gone back to his unit. In the turmoil and crises of war, the departure of the living or the dead was not a thing to be commented on.

For Macha to be Mark Connor was easy. She was tall and thin, and the years of physical work on the farm had made her strong and wiry. Her skill with the rifle silenced any who may have questioned her.

We know that Macha was on Crete, her documents showed this. The rest can only be conjecture – a story constructed from the way Macha behaved when she came back to her own town.

Crete for Macha would have been fairytale country, with its pine trees, green valleys and snow-capped mountains. A place from the books of myths and stories that Brigid had read to her when she was small.

One day, slow-moving German planes flew over the island, dropping paratroopers into the dreaming landscape. Down they floated like confetti in the bright sunlight, into the battle for Crete.

Maybe it was Macha's need for solitude that had made her climb a tree at the edge of a small inland village. Had her troop stopped here, and left her behind when they moved on? Rules never did concern Macha much, and she could well have walked away. Whatever the reason, there she was high up a tall pine, with an eagle's-eye view of the German soldiers entering the village. She watched the photographer snapping here, there and everywhere as women and children were pulled from their homes. She heard the commander shouting at the people as they lined up against the timber wall of their church. She heard a child whimper and saw a woman clasp her hand over the child's mouth. Too late, the man had a scapegoat: he pulled the child from her mother and pushed her onto her knees. He wanted information. The townspeople did not want to give it. No-one moved.

Macha saw the officer take his pistol from its holster. There was no reaction from the villagers, who could have been ancient statues in their impassiveness. The man held the weapon to the child's head, shouted the question again. Then pulled the trigger. The photographer, too, kept shooting.

Still no-one spoke to the commander. He signalled, and his troops herded the people into the church. A soldier poured liquid from a large can, dousing the door and the base of the wall. The commander struck a match and flames flew up the old wall.

Maybe Macha, in reaction to the horror, made a gagging noise and closed her eyes for a moment. This would have been too close. Killing, for her, was distanced by the sight cross-hairs of a powerful rifle. She looked again and there was the photographer walking through the pines. Towards her tree. As he walked he aimed the camera around him: left, right, ahead, upwards. Upwards, and there was an Australian soldier with a rifle aimed at him. Camera and gun faced each other. Hans dropped the camera and held up his hands in the classic position of surrender; but it was too late. Macha had squeezed the trigger. At the same moment, machine-gun fire cut down the women and children trying to escape the flames in the church of this small village deep in the Cretan countryside.

Macha swung her rifle towards the village, aimed at the back of the man with the machine-gun and pulled the trigger. As the man fell she shot the commander, who was waving his troops towards the pine forest. But Macha was down the tree, had picked up the camera from the pool of blood around the dead photographer, and was well away before the startled troops had reached the edge of the trees. She ran to a sobbing tune in her head. *The whole town. The whole town. The whole town.*

The houses on the outside streets of Siddon Rock turned their faces towards the town centre and their backs to the bush. Maureen Mather lived in one of these houses, one that had ramps, and doorways altered so she could move her wheelchair easily between house and garden.

The Mathers' backyard, like all those bordering the town edge, had a high back fence made of pickets nailed close together to form a solid wall and as much of a civilised garden as the indifferent rainfall and scorching summer sun would allow. Maureen's grandmother had started the plantings some sixty years before when the fence had been made of brush cut from the surrounding bush and tied with wire. The grandmother said that she could not sleep peacefully with the wild bush so close to her bedroom window, and that the fence at least gave a semblance of control over her home. She was also the first woman in the Mather family to see a wild woman squatting on the fence who, she said to the one or two women she could tell such things to, seemed to have two faces and could look in two directions at the same time, as if she was trying to decide whether to jump into the enclosed yard or out into the wild bush.

Since Maureen was two years old she knew the woman as part of the landscape and had no need to comment on her appearances. Macha Connor was the only other person who saw the wild woman. She said to Maureen that one day Maureen would have to help the woman decide which way to jump. Maureen just laughed. *She's been there forever*, she said. *Nothing will change.*

Late one night Maureen couldn't sleep and wheeled her chair onto the back verandah. From beyond the back fence came a foreign sound. At first Maureen thought it was a kangaroo, but the steps were too short for that bounding animal. As the noise came closer it resolved into the dragging tread of a long, slow walk of someone, or something, in the laneway between her back fence and the bush.

In Barber's Butchery & Bakery the next day Maureen paused to chat with Sybil, and mentioned the footsteps of the night before. Martha Hinks heard them talking. *I heard something*, she said. *It was like nothing I've ever heard before.*

The strange footsteps continued each night, and the stories quickly gathered momentum and size as the town discussed the mystery. Matron Helith, who had just arrived to take Matron Sullivan's place, asked Nell if she had any idea what it could be, but Nell was so surprised at being asked a question that she just shook her head and looked at the floor. Matron persisted, talking about stories of bunyips and unknown animals, but Nell mumbled something that sounded like *dream* and refused to say more. When Matron passed this on, it incensed Martha Hinks, who remarked tartly that she had certainly not been dreaming, and had most definitely heard the footsteps. How this was possible was uncertain as the Hinks family lived a good half block from the edge of town, but no-one challenged the comment.

Some of the old-timers remembered other darker stories from their parents' parents, and they wondered aloud about Aboriginal wild magic. Harry Best nipped this smartly in the bud by writing an article for the *District Examiner & Journal* which proved that this was impossible, *given that there are no tribes, as such, left in the state.* And anyway, everyone knew that there was no such thing as magic, wild or tame.

Maureen listened carefully to the noise for some nights. It was, she thought, like the exhausted march of battle-weary soldiers she had heard during the war. There were only two people she knew who would walk like that: her father Peter, who left the house only to go sit near the fire at the pub, and Macha Connor. She decided to challenge the treader and one night, as the dragging footsteps reached their loudest, from the verandah she called, *Who goes there?*

in a strong voice. There was no pause by the treader, and the sound quickly died away.

The next night she wheeled herself to the small cumquat tree that grew just inside the back gate. The trunk of this tree had grown spiralled around another, older, tree trunk; a eucalyptus of some sort which was now dead but still supported the cumquat. With help from her father to do the top clipping, Maureen was able to keep this small tree trimmed into a round mass of leaves. She had seen cumquats shaped like this in a large tub at the doorway of a London home, and liked the effect. Now, in the moonlight, the tree appeared insubstantial and weak. As the footsteps approached, Maureen gripped the arms of the wheelchair. *Who goes there?* she called. *Macha Connor, is that you?* The footsteps faltered, nearly stopped, and then resumed their tramping rhythm.

On the third night, Maureen again wheeled herself to the cumquat tree, and as the footsteps approached she threw off her blanket and heaved herself from the chair and onto the hard earth. *Macha. Macha Connor. I need your help*, she shouted. The footsteps slowed and then stopped and Maureen heard a shuffle and a breaking of twigs. *The back gate's open*, she called, making her voice weak and tearful. *I've fallen. Please help me up.* The gate-latch rattled and stuck for a moment, the gate creaked open and Macha marched in, her hat low over her face and the rifle at the slope. She stood over Maureen for a moment, then leaned the rifle against the cumquat tree and lifted Maureen carefully back into the chair, tucking the blanket firmly around her. She picked up the rifle and turned to go.

Would you like to hear a story? Maureen said. *I'd really like you to stay with me for a while.* Macha hesitated, and turned back. She closed the gate, and stood stiffly with rifle-butt resting on the ground, *looking for all the world*, Maureen thought, *like a bare tree in winter.* Maureen recalled a child's poem that her mother had told her, and this is what she recited to Macha, that night under the cold moon of July:

> *You think I am dead,*
> *The apple tree said,*
> *Because I have never a leaf to show –*
> *Because I stoop,*
> *And my branches droop,*
> *And the dull mosses over me grow.*
> *But I'm all alive in trunk and shoot;*
> *The buds of next May*
> *I fold away –*
> *You think I am dead,*
> *The pale grass said,*
> *Because I am brown and look so sad.*
> *But under the ground*
> *I am safe and sound,*
> *With the earth's thick blanket over me laid.*
> *I'm all alive and ready to shoot*
> *Should the spring of the year*
> *Come dancing here –*

At the pause Macha lifted the rifle smartly to slope position, and opened the gate. Maureen desperately searched her memory for the next verse of the poem.

You think I am dead/The earthworm said . . . No. Wait, Macha, I'll remember it in a moment.

You think I am dead/The grey goose said . . . bugger it, Macha, wait a bit. Give me a chance . . . For I cannot stay and I fly away, Maureen improvised.

Macha stepped into the lane but paused and looked back, and Maureen could swear that she saw a flicker behind the gaze that seemed to be looking to the far distance. When the gate closed behind Macha there was a long silence, and then the dragging tread resumed.

From this night on, when she couldn't sleep Maureen would wheel herself to the back fence and call to Macha as she passed. At first she did not stop, but it soon became a habit for Macha to open the back gate and wait by the cumquat tree whether Maureen was there or not. Gradually Maureen told pieces of Macha's own story. *Hey, Mach*, she'd say. *Remember that day when the recruitment march came? And what was it the recruitment bloke said when you wanted to sign up? 'We don't allow women to carry weapons.' And there you were, the best shot in the district, being told to stay home!*

And d'ya remember – there was that bloody cousin of yours, Fatman Aberline, signing himself for the airforce. And he laughed! The bastard laughed when he heard you couldn't even join the rifles. He always was jealous of you.

As a child, Fatman Aberline had loved the wild Macha with a passion that would horrify her, had she known of it. His envy was for her abilities and her freedom.

Fatman Aberline wanted to leave the polished calm imposed on his home by his mother Mabel, and the ordered control of his father Boy, and live in the chaos of Brigid's house. He wanted to have Brigid's rough kindness, as Macha did. He wanted to behave as he wished and have the town say of him, *Well, what do you expect from someone who's had no upbringing?* And, *dragged up, that's what she is.* But what the town saw as neglect Fatman knew was freedom, and Macha's abilities proved it.

Each time Fatman ran away from his own home and arrived at the Two Mile Brigid would drop whatever she was doing and ring Boy and Mabel. Often Fatman would stay for a day or so, but there were those times when an angry Boy Aberline would arrive within the hour and bundle Fatman into the truck and back home. Brigid said to Granna that she talked until she was blue in the face, but, no matter what, the child just kept turning up like a bad penny and causing trouble between her and his parents.

The boy wants to be Macha, Granna said. *He's got a free spirit being scrubbed away by that Mabel and her prissy husband.*

Whatever the problems between Brigid and Boy Aberline over his son, the rivalry between the cousins pushed Macha to drive faster, shoot further, ride the unbroken horse, in her determination to show her grandfather he was wrong when he said she was not-a-boy.

Mellor Mackintosh, the farmhand employed by Thomas Aberline to help his son's pregnant wife after his son walked away into the desert, stayed on the farm for five years and became the first of a long line of loving workers to share the bed of Brigid Connor. It seems that his farming background was mainly that of the buck-jumping ring on the Country Show circuit where he demonstrated riding and shooting to awed young farmers. It was he who taught Macha how to use the .22 rifle that was kept on the verandah, resting the long barrel on a box so that the small girl could steady it. *Tuck it in tight to ya shoulder*, he said. *Ya look at what ya aiming at through the rear sight, and then move the barrel up or down until it lines up with the foresight. Look through the target. You see and don't see at the same time.*

By the age of five Macha found she could see things that were obscured for others. *A veritable hawk*, her grandfather said to Brigid. *Shame she's not a boy*. Macha, who was lying on the cool earth under the verandah listening to them talk, wondered what he meant. She asked her cousin Fatman why she was not a boy, and he showed her the difference. *Well*, Macha said, *that's nothing special*, and at that moment she decided she would do all the things Fatman did, and do them so well that her grandfather would not know she was not-a-boy.

By the time she was twelve Macha Connor could out-ride anyone in the district and could dismantle and re-assemble any piece of machinery known. But her prime skill was with the rifle.

Saw her pick an eagle's eye at five hundred yards, Billy Brody said over a schooner in the bar. Billy had only been at the Two Mile for a month or two (Mellor Mackintosh was long gone) and was still able to be surprised by the abilities of the Connor women. *As for rabbits – the bloody things stop at the fence line 'cause they know they'll be dead meat otherwise.* And rabbit was indeed a staple on the table at the Two Mile.

↣

. . . Just fancy that, those bloody idiots at the recruitment table would only let you enlist as a nurse – but I'm glad we got to be together for a while at least, just the two of us from Siddon Rock, Maureen said. *And I'm glad you got to do what you wanted to do. You're so good at it – and maybe one day you'll be able to tell me about it.* But Maureen Mather, thinking about her father's restless nights and sullen days that had been with him since 1918, knew this would not happen.

PART TWO

CHAPTER SIX
CATALIN AND JOS ARRIVE

There are those who say it was Macha Connor
who disturbed things, but most lay it on Catalin
Morningstar.

CATALIN MORGENSTERN walked out of the migrant camp one afternoon with her small suitcase in one hand and the other holding her son Josis. They were accompanied only by the ghosts. The cello case was on her back, as it always was when she travelled. No-one thought to ask where she was going, and if they had she could not have told them.

At the railway station she saw that the trains were older than the ones she had travelled on in Germany, older and not as clean, even without the veneer of war. But the smell of the station – the coal and steam from the engines – was the same. Here though, there were no uniforms checking every passenger; in fact, there seemed to be no-one at all worrying about who got on or off the trains.

Catalin watched which trains had travellers with luggage, and she chose one being loaded with cases of food and packages, and with two other passengers in a small carriage at the rear. She sat with the cello, the suitcase and Josis, and no-one asked if she had permission to travel, or a ticket. For the rest of that day she did not speak for fear of being discovered.

By nightfall they were alone on the train, but when the engine uncoupled and steamed off into the night Catalin was not afraid that they had been left. The food boxes and packages had not been unloaded, and she knew they were not at the end of the journey.

The stillness, though, allowed the ghosts to expand, and they hung there below the ceiling, whispering things that Catalin did not want to hear or remember. She put her hands over Josis's ears so he would not be frightened, but when he wriggled away she realised that he could not hear them, that these ghosts were hers alone.

While Josis slept against her, she sat watching the turn of the stars in a silence of such depth and darkness as she had never known. It felt, she thought, as if the continent itself was hiding from her. In the deepest dark just before dawn, an engine steamed backwards to the waiting carriages, coupled, and continued the journey.

Catalin and Jos sat for much of the next day, watching the landscape become flatter and browner. Jos, who rarely spoke, pointed at kangaroos bounding alongside the train, as if challenging to a race; or to strange, red-coloured trees that grew with all the leaves at the top of their tall trunks. When the train stopped at the siding before Siddon Rock, Catalin stood to get off, thinking that they were surely far enough from the capital to not be found. She had been dozing, sitting with her feet tucked under her on the seat, away from the wind blowing through the gap under the carriage door. As she stood her toes pushed backwards, cramping against each other. She lifted her foot and dug her thumb into the unnatural hollow where the muscle compressed above the little toe and its companion, rubbing and gasping at the betrayal of her body. The train moved off before she had time to even look out the window.

Shortly after, the train stopped again. Catalin looked out to see a row of shops and a hotel, and she and Jos stepped down into Siddon Rock. As they stood in the gravel of the station-yard she felt the blue heat lean heavily on her head, pushing her into the earth. She took a step or two after the train, but it was already moving. She watched it diminishing and for some minutes she could hear the slow *tuggetty-tuk* of the wheels and feel the rhythm in her body.

That night in the small room in the hotel, Catalin took the cello from its case. She held it to the light and rubbed her fingers over the words that were written on the front of the instrument, flowing in an ongoing line around the edge like an intricate decoration. Near the top where the neck joined the body the words had, with time, worn so low that she was unable to decipher many of them, but the last names stood clearly:

> *Margit Catalin 1879 to 1930 . . . Viktoria Margit . . .*
> *Catalin Viktoria . . . Josis Matthieu . . .*

Her fingers lingered on the space after the words *Viktoria Margit*, and the smoothness made her smile. She turned the cello over to look at the back, which was covered by a seeming jumble of overlapping painted scenes of cities and countryside. Interspersed were intimate details: a right hand with a particularly beautiful ring on the middle finger; an unusually styled red boot; an opened fan that almost fluttered off the cello, so real it appeared; a silver teaspoon with a twining pattern on the handle.

At the place where the neck of the cello joined the body, there were small pictures of several women. Catalin found her grandmother's face and touched it gently. She was a child when her grandmother died, and had no memory of her. She wished she could have known her.

Catalin's mother's picture was not yet there for she was, as the words at the edge of the cello told her daughter, still alive.

Catalin propped the cello against the wall and stepped back so that the details of the painting were not so clear, and a sense of wholeness flowed towards her from the instrument.

That first night, Catalin slept with Josis curled against her back. Her dreams had no uniforms, running figures or gunfire, but she woke some time in the grey of pre-dawn with a profound feeling of unease. The shadows in the hotel room reminded her of the dream that had stirred her, and she recalled its nothingness, its world filled with white light that flowed over her with no sense of peace, and stretched forever.

Macha Connor sat with Nell on the steps of the war memorial, her hand on the head of one of the dingoes, watching the train enter the town and draw to a bumping, grinding halt.

A woman climbed down the steps of the dog-box carriage carrying a small suitcase and a large cello case. Macha did not see the small boy jump down behind her, but only the army of dark ghosts that floated out of the train around the woman, almost lifting her off the ground as they crowded close. Some wore uniforms of the German or Allied Forces, some had only rags drifting from vaporous figures, and they ebbed and flowed around her like a black tide.

The dog under Macha's hand stirred and its hackles lifted as one of the dark shapes detached from the group and drifted towards them. Macha picked up her rifle. Nell looked at the dog, and then at Macha who stood trembling with her finger tightening on the trigger. *Hey, Mach,* she said, *whatcha doin'? You can't kill someone else's ghosts.*

Macha lowered the rifle, slung it over her shoulder and walked quickly away down Wickton Street, gaining speed until she broke into a trot and then a run. She rushed past the pub, where Kelpie Crush was sweeping broken glass off the steps of the bar; past the bank and the Council Offices, and vanished up the path over the rock.

When Catalin and Josis appeared in the doorway of the pub, Bluey Redall called to Marge, who led them to a bedroom and then to the bathroom.

After an hour Marge Redall went upstairs again. *Got something to eat in the kitchen*, she said, and they followed her to where she had set two places at the huge work-table. *What's yer name, love?* she asked as she ladled beef and barley soup into large bowls. Catalin hesitated, wanting to protect herself and her son, but not wanting to lie to this woman. *Morningstar*, she said. *This is the closest, is English. I am Catalin, and this is Josis.*

Here'ya, young Joe. Marge gave him the bowl of soup.

Not Joe, Jo-sis, Catalin said as she opened her bag and tipped some coins on the table, pushing them towards Marge.

Don't be silly, love. Marge pushed them back. *Let's wait and see what happens.*

Catalin returned them. *I pay*, she said. *I work.* Marge Redall looked at the slightly built woman, and at the boy who had taken his bowl of soup to sit close to her, and wondered just what she would work at in Siddon Rock. *As you like*, she said and put a couple of pennies in her apron pocket.

The next day Marge took Catalin and Jos to Meakins' Haberdashery and Ladies & Men's Apparel. *Now this ain't charity, love, and you can pay what you can*, she said. *But you've gotta have some clothes for young Jos.* She had seen the one tiny case and guessed the rest. *On my account*, she muttered to Alistair Meakins. When Catalin put a five-pound note on the counter to pay for a shirt and shorts for Jos and a dress and some underwear for herself, Alistair took it and put it in the till, then he gave her back a mix of notes and silver that more than equalled the note she had given him.

Without looking, Catalin put it in her bag. Much later, when most barriers had been dismantled, Alistair asked Catalin if she had known how to count Australian money at that time. *Yes*, she said, *but I knew you were trusty*. She didn't tell him that in her experience, violet-coloured people were usually timid, and liked to be liked.

Catalin saw the world as various colours, and the days of the week of Siddon Rock were very differently coloured from the days of the week in Germany, or those in the camp at the capital. Take Tuesday. In Berlin this was a pale icy-green with smudgy white edges; in the camp it was still green, although much darker; but here in this small town in the middle of who-knows-where, it was a deep russet. Wednesday was pale pink and Saturday a spiritual and glorious blue. She found, however, that if she focused her eyes in a certain way, by looking at a point at the tip of her nose, she could see familiar colours just under the veneer, so that Siddon Rock Friday orange barely concealed Berlin Friday ecru; and the deep purple of a Hungarian Sunday flashed under the Siddon Rock red.

But Catalin had no problem with the colours of the place; it was the people who seemed to be uniformly brown, except for Alistair Meakins, and Marge Redall who glowed like a silvery-blue beacon in the forest. *But there is no forest*, Catalin thought. *Nothing but nothingness.*

Catalin and Jos were hovering at the edge of the town, where the track went around the silo and up the rock, when

Kelpie Crush walked up behind them. *You can go up*, he said, *it's quite safe*. But Catalin recoiled from his dark grey presence. She saw, too, that when he spoke to her he had a blue and smiling eye, but when he turned and looked back at her from the path ahead, a sharp, gingery glare shone from an eye that looked like that of a fox. She hurried back to the town centre.

Two weeks after their arrival, Catalin was surprised by the knock at the door of her hotel room, and even more so to see the pale lemony-coloured shape that was Matron Helith of the Siddon Rock and District Hospital. Within a few minutes Catalin was hired to work as a wardsmaid and kitchen relief. She was to have a large room with a small room off it, *quite suitable for yourself and the child*. Catalin would use the hospital kitchen to cook meals for herself and Jos, and would cook for patients and staff when Nell was not there. *Nell has been with us longer than anyone can remember*, said Matron Helith.

The Siddon Rock and District Hospital stood at the north-east corner of the town, surrounded by pale greyish earth. Catalin had seen many exotic buildings on her rambling journey from Budapest to Berlin to Siddon Rock, but she stopped in stunned amazement at the awkwardness, the sheer, unbelievable excess of the hospital building. It stood high off the ground, spread with three equally spaced wings leading from a small central block, all balanced on what looked, to Catalin, like leafless trees. *Like a spaceship*,

Catalin would say later when telling the story of her arrival. Matron Helith laughed at Catalin's reaction.

The only builder anywhere in the district was a bloke from Queensland, she said. *Members of the Council all looked at the plans, but everyone just assumed that it would be the same sort of building as everything else here. It wouldn't have mattered anyway, as he only knew how to put up stilt houses. It does keep very cool, though.*

And indeed, as Catalin walked into the central area where the three corridors met, there was a distinct drop in temperature. Such a different hospital this was, from the crowded and dirty room where Jos had been born among the death and detritus of war. Here there were no uniformed men with vacated eyes, no urgency to give birth and leave. Here in the cocooned world of healing it was as if the outside world of hot wind and dust did not exist.

That night Catalin looked for paper to write on, to record her first day at her new job. She found the local newspaper, the *District Examiner & Journal*. The back page was headed 'Classified Advertisements' but there was nothing but a large white space. In this Catalin wrote: *I am in a bad dream. Tonight, this first night in this place, I want to make Jossy feel good, to feel at home in all this strangeness. So I go to the kitchen to make an omelette, like he likes, or maybe a potato latke. But where are the small implements, the sauté pans, to do this. I think I am in the land of giants where I am too small, and overwhelmed by everything. Everywhere there are enormous pots, huge saucepans in which two or three eggs or a grated potato would disappear – like the country, so big that it eats up everything. And how many people are there here to need such huge saucepans? This is such a small town, how many people could there be in the wards?*

And there is a ghost called Nell in the kitchen. I see her, but she has no colour – she should not be here, but in her own place, which is not this building, so her colour waits for her at home. She tells me that people in this town do not see her at all, except when she is at work here at the hospital, or at her other work cleaning the school.

As for Nell, she realised that Catalin was one of those people who are able to slip across borders, but had yet to learn the language of this place.

Later, Matron Helith told Catalin that the huge pots were bought by the first matron of the hospital. There had been high expectations that a population of new settlers with large families would take up land, and so the hospital had been built and supplied accordingly. Instead, the marginal rainfall and barren salt-prone ground made farming difficult, and the district and town did not grow. She told this when she was showing Catalin through the three corridors of the hospital.

In the first corridor, high-ceilinged rooms were darkened by drawn blinds. Beds held bare mattresses covered with a rubber sheet, and metal trolleys were angled neatly over the bed-ends waiting to hold meal trays and medications. Next to them standard hospital bedside cupboards stood open. The wide corridor had heavy doors at each end, muffling external noises. There was a feeling of dulled expectancy. *Never been used*, Matron Helith said.

Terrible waste it is. Was to be the maternity ward, for all the new little ones. But it never happened. There's a small four-bed ward in the main corridor that we use for mums and bubs, that's more than enough. Much easier for one night-nurse to handle, too.

The second corridor was the nurses' quarters and empty except for the rooms given to Catalin and her son, as staff were generally drawn from the young women of the town. The third corridor held separate wards for men, women and children, each with six beds, and the small maternity ward of four beds.

There was one room, away from the others, where a dull light shone through the half-closed door, and Catalin could see murky grey and dark green colours hanging like dirty cobwebs around a large metal cylinder. A sound like ghostly bellows filled the room. *Ah yes, Young Ralphie*, Matron Helith said. *Poor little blighter. He'll always be here. Polio.* Catalin understood the colours then. *Stagnation, confinement, death.*

Catalin hugged Jos hard when she put him to bed that night. She said goodnight and checked the names on the edge of the cello:

Margit Catalin 1879 to 1930 . . . Viktoria Margit . . .
Catalin Viktoria . . . Josis Matthieu . . .

Then she stood the instrument in the corner of the room, opposite the bed so that Jos could see the pictures painted on it. *To keep away the beasties*, she said. That night she slept fitfully, trying to ignore the wisps of grey and murky green floating past her window. *I will not run again*, she wrote on the back of an envelope. *This must be home.*

Bluey Redall talked often with Catalin when she was living at the pub. One night when Harry Best beat him at poker, Bluey challenged him, the headmaster of Siddon Rock Primary School, that Catalin Morningstar would take his crown as town intellectual. Harry demurred, saying that he had seen no signs of this when she enrolled the boy at the school. But the comment intrigued him, and he would watch Catalin as she walked down Wickton Street to the small lending library at the Council Offices and back to the hospital. She rarely had a book with her, and Harry knew the few shelves contained mainly popular fiction and some children's books.

One day Harry followed her and Jos as they climbed the track winding up the rock. He called to them and was shocked by their reaction. *Like startled rabbits*, he told the poker players. *Took off down the rock faster'n bloody lightning.*

Ya want me to introduce ya? Bluey Redall offered. *As long as I can be there when she wipes the floor with ya!*

Intro, yes. Be there, no. Harry was adamant, using his headmaster's voice. *I want to find out if she's suitable to talk to the kids. About where she comes from and what her country's like. Maybe she can tell them about living in a war. And you hanging around won't help at all.*

And so it came about that one evening Catalin Morningstar left Jos with Marge Redall in the pub kitchen, and met Harry Best in the Ladies' Lounge of the Railway and Traveller's Hotel. There they engaged in the first round of mind-dances that would last for many years.

Mrs Morningstar, Harry started. *My apologies for calling to you on the rock. I didn't mean to frighten you.*

It's Miss Morningstar. I am not married, Catalin replied. *You don't frighten me. No-one frightens me. It's your colours, they are so mixed and bright. I can't look at you without it hurts my eye.*

So I'm a bright lad, am I? Harry Best quipped, but with no response from Catalin. *Shall I sit under the table, then? So your eyes are not offended?*

Catalin did not smile. *That would be quite acceptable. Then we can talk.*

What colour am I? Harry asked, from beneath the tablecloth.

A bright purpley-red, Catalin said. *What IS this drink called? And you have streaks of orange.*

A shandy. Do the colours signify anything? Do they mean I am something particular?

I know what 'signify' means, Catalin snapped. *It's just that I see people as colours. No reason. I just do. Other things too. Your sound is not the colour of your look – it is confusing. And may I please have a scotch whisky with some water. This is the very worst thing I have ever tasted in a glass.*

Only if I can have one with you – above table. Shut your eyes for a moment.

Harry went to Kelpie Crush, who was pulling beers in the main bar. When he returned to the table, balancing a round tray on one hand, he took a pair of sunglasses from his pocket and handed them to Catalin. *Here's protection*, he said. He put down two glasses of Johnnie Walker scotch. *Here's the drinks.* Then a small jug of water. *Here's the dilutant. And here's something if we need to cool things off*, and he placed on the table a bowl of ice-cubes that Kelpie had given him from the kitchen fridge. *Now can we talk?*

Catalin laughed, and it was a sound like no-one had heard before in Siddon Rock. A belly-laugh which rolled out in rich, scarlet waves, so that even the men in the bar – separated by a closed door, a corridor, another door, and the tall back of the bottle shelf – were transfixed by the splendour of it, the sheer, deep and suggestive beauty of it. Nell, walking near the railway station, smiled to hear the sound and then laughed with Catalin, and the dogs following her joined in. Marge Redall, spooning soup into a bowl for Catalin's son in the kitchen, also smiled, and then shuddered as black imps of mischief tumbled through the door on the sound. *Hey, Kelpie*, she called. *Come 'n' watch young Joe for a sec.* And she marched into the Ladies' Lounge, knowing that it was all too late.

In the kitchen Kelpie Crush smiled at Jos and handed him a glass of lemonade. *Here you are, young Joe*, he said. *We don't need to tell your mum about this, do we? Marge and Bluey won't mind you having a drink.*

The short-term outcome of the meeting between Harry Best, headmaster of Siddon Rock Primary School, and Catalin Morningstar, holder of a doctorate in science from the University of Budapest, was that Catalin went to the primary school to tell the Grades 5 and 6 something about Europe.

The long-term result of the meeting was one that only three people ever knew about, apart from Catalin and Harry themselves. Harry's wife came to know because one day a piece of water-pressed paper fell from a pocket as she hung laundry on the line. The visible letters of a few compressed words told her some, but not enough, and she decided there and then that unless she was shamed in front of the town she would not watch them and would say nothing. What could a woman of her middle-years and inexperience do to make a living?

Nell, who cleaned the school each afternoon when she finished at the hospital, knew; but then she always saw more than the town realised.

Granna, of course, knew.

Later, when people wondered out loud to Catalin why she, such an attractive if somewhat unusual woman, had not married she always replied, *I have had only one love in my life, and cannot possibly marry.*

CHAPTER SEVEN

THE DAY HITLER VISITED SIDDON ROCK

It don't matter where you end up, it's just not possible to leave the old place behind. You learn everything in the place of your childhood.

BERLIN IS – WAS – A VERY BEAUTIFUL CITY, Catalin said to the crowded classroom of children. *It had beautiful buildings that had been there for nearly a thousand years.* But *a thousand years* was not a concept available to these children of this new place, and incomprehension dulled their listening.

Think about this place here, where you live. What about the rock? The rock has been there for many, many thousands of years. And the people who were here before you came. Think about them.

But, said one young Aberline, *there were no people here before we came.*

Yes, said Catalin, *the Aboriginal people. All the tribes.*

The next day Gloria Aberline and Martha Hinks knocked on Harry Best's door. They asked him why this New Australian thought she knew more about Australian history than they themselves did.

Berlin was a very beautiful city, Catalin told the small faces watching her. *It has – it had – wide avenues. Twice as wide as Wickton Street to the railway station*. The child of the station-master asked why it did not have them now.

The English and American bombs have broken them down, she said.

An angry Mister Placer closed the railway station at lunch-time and banged into Harry Best's office, demanding to know why this ignorant Balt was telling them lies about our fighting boys.

I lived in Berlin, Catalin said. *I used to teach at a university there.* A child timidly asked why she had left. She told them, *I had to leave because the Nazis were killing my friends.*

Gentle Gawain Evans stopped Harry Best in the street, wanting to know how he could allow such brutality to be talked about in his school.

What would you like me to talk about with you? Catalin asked the class.

My dad said you're a Hun and I should ask you what you did in the war, Miss? The voice was disguised and the class giggled nervously.

I'll tell you a story, Catalin said. She turned the room into a dark cavern by pulling down the window-blinds, and switched on the light on the teacher's desk, placing it so that it threw a bright arc on the wall. *Once when it was not*, she began, *beyond seven times seven countries and the sea of Operencia, behind an old stove in a crack in the wall in the skirt of an old hag, and there in the seven times seventh fold – a white flea, and in the middle of it the beautiful city of a king.*

Now this king had been taking care of the beautiful city for many years, and he ruled in the same way that his father had, and his father's father had, and all the fathers back as far as anyone could remember. However, there were some who lived there who called him a 'slow old dog'. Catalin held her hands together in front of the light and on the wall appeared the shadow of a dog's head with ears cocked forward, opening and closing its mouth. The children laughed.

One day a wolf came to the beautiful city. The dog shadow appeared again, but this time it looked larger and the mouth was more open, showing its teeth. *At first the people thought this wolf was their friend* – in her voice were sounds of laughing and cheering, and on the wall tiny figures appeared to be waving – *and they welcomed him and said that he could bring his friends to stay.* Small wolf-shadows mixed with the people-shadows on the wall. *For a while they all lived together happily. The old-dog king even asked the wolf and his friends to visit him at the palace, and they talked of this and that, but mainly about the people and the kingdom.*

There came a time, though, when there was famine in the beautiful city and people began to say that the old-dog king was too old and ill to rule, and that maybe the wolf and his friends should rule in his place.

And so the wolf went to the king and told him that he would look after the problem of the famine, because the king had been so welcoming to them and had given them a home. The wolf and his friends went out among the hungry people but instead of giving them bread, they had lists of names and guns with them. Catalin moved her hands in front of the light and more wall-shadows appeared, of running people being rounded up by wolves. Her voice held the thud of marching boots and gunfire. *This is just like your sheep-dogs do with your sheep, eh? Round them into pens so they can be sorted out and taken away.* And the people-shadows huddled in one corner of the wall, surrounded by wolves. *But these wolves call out some people's names and not others, so that the ones not called are very pleased. They tell the wolves the names of the others they think should be taken away, so that they themselves will be allowed to stay.*

Who had to go, Miss? Angie Aberline asked. *How did the wolves choose?*

Ah, Catalin said, and the wall shadows became larger and moved more wildly, *now that was the question, wasn't it? Who indeed?* A keening sound that could have been the plovers crying from near the cemetery filled the room. *All these people seem the same, don't they? But the wolves thought not; they thought that some were making the beautiful city an impure city, so this is what happened.* The wall darkened as it became a mass of shifting shadows, which separated into many wolves and a few people. *The people who the wolves didn't like had different types of names from their own. They looked different from those people who joined the wolves. Maybe they were Gypsy or Jewish people. Maybe they thought that a different family of wolves should control the beautiful city. But always the first wolf said who could stay and who had to be sent away or killed.* Many voices shouting filled the room, all shouting the same two words that sounded like *see hail*, and the wolves became more frantic, snapping and biting at the few people left.

Someone in the class laughed. Catalin spun around. *So. So you think this is a funny story.* She stopped talking and turned to the wall. Light flooded the room, and the wolf-shadows grew and spread, a great dark stain across the whiteness of the walls, until they filled all four walls of the classroom. The *thump-thump* of many marching feet, mixed with the sound of breaking glass and gunfire, was loud and threatening. Black wolf-shapes slid from the wall to the floor making children scream and stand on their desks. Behind the spreading shadows in the room, dressed in a uniform that tucked into long boots, stood the largest wolf of all, so large that he filled a wall on his own. He held his arm straight out in front of him and flames engulfed the shadow-world and burned the few remaining people-shapes. When there were none left the wolf leaped from the wall into the schoolroom, running at the children and dragging flames with him until the dry timber of the room itself started to burn. Children screamed and ran for the door, which appeared to be jammed shut until Catalin opened it and let them outside. *It's good to be able to get out, isn't it?* she said. *Not like the people in the beautiful city, eh.*

The children, even in their old age, when asked what had happened the day the schoolhouse caught on fire, just shrugged and said they didn't really remember, not wishing to drag the shame of that day from the deepest shadows of their memories. But many years later, when he was in a position of immense power in the government of the nation, one in particular remembered and said *no* at a crucial moment.

That night, Catalin, in the margins of an old copy of the *District Examiner & Journal*, wrote:

> If I could be dying
> Sand in my nose, eyes
> Fighting the tongue for space
> I'd rather.

Some people live as if they have forgotten death, Catalin said to Macha as she walked with her on the nightly patrol around the borders of the town. This was after Jos disappeared, for Catalin would not have left him alone at night. Not ever.

CHAPTER EIGHT

SIDDON ROCK SUNDAY

The things that drive people are generally well hidden. They surge along beneath the surface of the spirit, and only pop up at extreme times.

ON HER DAILY WALK Catalin passed all houses of worship in the town: the solid-looking Roman Catholic church that stood, squarely dark-brick, within a gravelled yard; the Church of England with its stained glass and frills of flowers and shrubs at the walls; and the small, weatherboard Methodist church that, although the first place of worship in the town, seemed neglected and in need of a good coat of paint.

Gloria Aberline and Martha Hinks stopped Catalin one day and invited her to attend a service at the Methodist church. Catalin smiled her most charming smile and said, *Thank you so much, but it is not possible.*

They must be Catholic, Martha Hinks muttered as they walked on.

The words may not have been exactly the same when the Roman Catholic priest called on Catalin at the hospital; nor when the vicar from the Church of England stopped her as they passed in Wickton Street one afternoon. But the message was clear: Catalin and Jos Morningstar did not attend any church.

Instead, Catalin took Jos to places that, she told him, *are much more spiritual than words written in a book by men.* Whenever it was possible – that is, when there were no patients in the hospital to cook for – on a Sunday they went either to the rock, where Jos would chase clouds of brown moths from the dark gullies where they hid from the light, or to the salt lake. Jos preferred the lake. He delighted in the fragile-looking dragonflies that skimmed the surface of the still water, and jumped away and laughed as pieces of stick transformed into gangly insects that moved awkwardly as they tried to keep the shape and colouration of the dead twigs they clung to. Not even the swarms of small bush flies worried him, although Catalin would sit in the shade waving a piece of paper or her hat to keep them away. Catalin relished these times for their quiet peacefulness.

This is such a different place, Catalin told Jos one Sunday. *We must get to know it, not just like this* – she waved her arm, indicating the town hidden by the rock behind them and the space that opened up across the salt lake to the inland – *but here, too* – she tapped herself over the heart, and then touched Jos on the head. *But it takes time, much time, although there is much time here, waiting to be used.*

Nell was eclectic in her Sunday morning routine. This started with her leaning against the brick wall of the

Catholic church as early mass was said, and she found a sort of bliss as the droning chants touched something within her that she couldn't quite remember. Then she went to Anglican morning prayer, which was, she felt, so similar to the Catholic sound that she sometimes wondered why the two mobs didn't sing together. Whichever one it was, she would shuffle the dust as she moved to the priest's or vicar's plainsong.

By the time the Anglicans received the benediction, the Methodists' service in the shabby weatherboard building around the corner was usually halfway through, so Nell had to sit out the end of the sermon. But she didn't mind the wait as she particularly enjoyed the complicated harmonies of the hymns, and often added a counter rhythm with two sticks tapped together. *Rock of ages, cleft for me,* she'd hum as she climbed the track past the silo and over the rock to her hut, *let me hide myself in thee.*

For these last several Sundays Nell found, as she sat on the step leading into the tiny vestibule of the Methodist church, that while she liked the hymns it was the sound of the sermons that held her attention. And apparently most of the congregation enjoyed them too, although it needs to be remembered that at the time this particular body of Christ numbered just some twenty-nine souls, if one counted the lapsers of the Aberline clan who rarely attended.

Good sermon today, Mister Butow. You should put them in a book, they'd say as hands were shaken and good wishes for the coming week murmured. *Making us think, that's what you're doing.* Or *Like the Bible sections you're using, Butow. Ecclesiasticus today, wasn't it?* And *Particularly liked today's burst, Siggy.*

Nell, out of sight of the departing Methodists, laughed to herself. She too *liked today's burst*, and thought that the Reverend Siggy Butow had these people fooled. The sound in his voice was just like that in the voice of Matron Sullivan before she died. *This man's voice*, she said to her dogs walking with her, *this old man's voice is telling them: You poor dumb people, waddya know about anything. Here, I'll tell you about it. Then you'll know.*

Near her shack Nell sat in the sparse shade of a clump of mallee and recalled the sermon, and she talked to her dingoes about the numbers of *today's burst*: 13, 15 and 17. *Nice shape*, Nell said to a dog panting at her side. She knew well the Bible quote, the mission school had made sure of that. This is what she remembered, and what she heard at the beginning of the sermon:

Every beast loveth his like, and every man loveth his neighbour. All flesh consorteth according to kind, and a man will cleave to his like. What fellowship hath the wolf with the lamb? What indeed. Nell roared with laughter until the dogs slunk away into the bush. She knew what these people thought this Mister Butow was telling them. They thought, and she laughed again, they thought that *they* were the lambs. But she, Nell, knew different. A picture of the late Matron Sullivan came to mind. *These people, these baby people, they think that my people are the wolves.* And the idea set her off into another paroxysm of mirth.

Then she remembered another service she had heard last month, when Abe Simmons and his wife stood at the front of the church holding their infant son, to name him in the sight of their god. This Mister Butow had no softness in his voice when he looked at the child, indeed his voice seemed louder and more emphatic than usual. *A firstborn bull*, he roared, *majesty is his! His horns are the horns of a wild ox; with them he gores the peoples, driving them to the ends of the earth.*

Searching among her memories from the mission school she found the right numbers: 33 and 17. It took a bit longer to find the name attached to the numbers, but eventually she did, the hard one to say, *Deuteronomy.*

Nell's laughing stopped and the dogs came back, tentatively sniffing the air around her. *How come this Mister Butow don't see that you can't be a lamb and a bull at the same time?* she said to them. *It's just too hard to try to think like those people.*

Later she told this to Granna, who said, *Those people, they think that putting the stories on a piece of paper makes 'em theirs, as if they won't ever change.*

That night Nell lit a small fire outside her hut and, when it was burning well, dropped some eucalyptus leaves onto it so that healing smoke drifted around her campsite and through the hut. Then she and the dogs slept.

Sybil Barber knew that Kelpie Crush was a tender and gentle cook. In her shop he always asked for lamb, or veal if it was in season. *Young and tender is how I like things*, he'd say regularly, as if this was a private joke between them. When she asked him what he did for the other ingredients – the Siddon Rock Farmers' Co-op being long on bags of sugar and flour but short on French herbs and spices – he said, *It's amazing what can be substituted. I just make it up as I go along.* After a while Sybil made a point of having a choice cut for him, or a fine chicken from one of the local farmers, when she thought she knew his tastes.

Kelpie, who rarely slept, sometimes cooked at night. Marge Redall would open the fridge to get eggs for breakfast, to find containers of food she was unable to name. Kelpie once offered her his French cuisine magazines, saying that there were some good recipes, but she waved them away. *Hey, Kelp,* she said, *if I started giving that mucky-looking stuff to the blokes in the bar I may as well shut up shop.*

On Sunday morning, when the pub was closed, Kelpie did most of his cooking and thinking. This particular Sunday, after he'd put the *coq au vin* in the oven and cleaned up the kitchen, he sat in the Strangers' Room with a small bourbon and soda, thinking about the Siddon Rock Cub Scouts Pack in general, and about young Jos Morningstar.

There was something vulnerable about young Jos, a softness and sweetness not seen in the tougher boys who had grown in the heat of the inland. He had first seen this in the kitchen on the evening that Harry Best met Catalin Morningstar, the night Catalin's laugh stunned the bar-leaners into silence and made her a person to be desired. The idea of Jos's gentle quality made Kelpie Crush smile, then pause and wonder if it would survive the heat generated by the boys in the pack, if he was to join. *A bit like trying to grow French tarragon in the outback*, he thought. *Some things just need more nurturing than others.*

As he ladled chicken and wine sauce into a bowl, Kelpie again saw the young boy at the table, holding his soup spoon in a manner that could never be natural to the boys of Siddon Rock, and decided then and there that he would invite Jos to join the pack even though he was younger than the official acceptance age. And he would take extra-special care of him, nurturing him so that he did not get too bruised and battered.

Here is a small part of the story of Kelpie Crush. A fragment of the things he held hidden in a locked room of his mind.

Kelpie's father, Garfield Crush, was what was once known as *a hard man*, meaning that he *took no lip from no-one*. This is what Kelpie remembered of the man who appeared to the child as a mountain among men: that he moved like a king among the rubbish-bins and low-life of the back-alleys of the capital. And no-one, not even the local coppers, ever *gave him lip*. He remembered, too – when he mounted the collection of moths and insects into likely seeming categories – a moment that was crystallised like amber in his memory. So clear it was, that he could feel the heat of the city evening through his shirt, and the smell and crunch of dry summer grass at the verge of the road. He saw the gigantic hands of Garfield catch a tiny white butterfly and drop it into his, Robert's, own hands and he felt the fluttering panic of the insect on the soft skin of his palms, and started to smile at the tickle of its wings.

Feel the life, Garfield said. *Feel the power in such a little thing.* Then he banged his hands against Kelpie's, smashing the butterfly between the child's palms. *That's the power we have to have*, Garfield said. *Ya gotta be the boss, otherwise ya get lip.*

Barber's Butchery & Bakery was, as the women of the town often said, *so spick and span that you could eat off the floor.* Indeed, Sybil spent many hours after closing the shop, and sometimes before opening, scrubbing and cleaning the walls, floor, pine benches and blocks.

It was Sunday morning, though, when the major weekly clean took place. Each Sunday, too, the shade of Alf Barber stood over her as she worked, commenting and remembering: *Your mother's at church, Sib, just you 'n' me at home. Good for a dad to have some time with his daughter, eh?* he'd start. Sybil concentrated on her scrubbing, ignoring the rough voice behind her. *Come on, luv,* he'd whisper, *come and sit with your dad for a minute. Remember how you'd sit on me knee? That was good, wasn't it?*

Sybil scoured harder and sang loudly – *Chickery chick, cha-la, cha-la, Check-a-la romey in a bananika* – as she filled a bucket with hot water, added a good dash of vinegar and started to sluice the chopping blocks, but each time her elbow moved backwards it entered Alf's shade, which weakened her arm until she could hardly move it. Sybil knew it was no use talking to him – reason was never a strong point for Alf Barber – and shouting just made him worse, but her anger built as she worked, pushing her faster and making her sing louder to block out Alf's insidious voice – *Bollika, wollika, can't you see, Chickery chick is me. Chickery chick, cha-la, cha-la . . .*

Come on Sib, what's the matter? Alf sounded as if a grave injustice was being done to him. *Ain't this mine? The shop, and you?*

. . . Check-a-la romey in a bananika, Bollika, wollika, can't you see, Chickery chick is me . . .

Alf Barber would raise his voice over the song, *A wife belongs to a man, and so do a daughter – and that's you. I c'n do what I like.*

Sybil scrubbed harder, banging the brush on the wooden countertop as if it were the enemy, lifting her voice to drown out her father's . . . *Once there lived a chicken who would say chick-chick chick-chick all day . . . oohhhh . . . chickery chick, cha-la, cha-la . . .*

And so it went: Sybil scrubbed and sang, not looking up, ignoring the pain in her body where it touched the shade of Alf Barber. Alf cajoled and pleaded.

After a while Alf's shade would lose his temper at being ignored and retreat to the corner where Alf used to dump the bones and off-cuts when he ran the shop. There it stood, hawking and spitting into the sawdust that covered the floor behind the counter, or throwing down the knives and saws that Sybil had just cleaned. Each time he did this Sybil would have to start again – soaking the knives in boiling water then scouring the blades with sandsoap before rinsing, sharpening and wiping on a thin film of oil to stop rust. After this the walls and countertops needed re-scrubbing as did the floor, which also had a clean layer of sawdust.

Eventually Alf Barber would tire of trying to seduce Sybil with words or tantrums, and float off out the back door, leaving Sybil to finish the weekly routine. But always, always there was the voice as she locked the door behind her on a Sunday. *I know you remember, Sib. I know you do.*

The problem was, she found she could never get the smell of Alf off her hands, no matter how long she scrubbed them or what soap or abrasive she used. When she told this to Catalin, well after they knew most of each other's stories, Catalin gave her a jar of cleanser that the hospital used in the operating theatre. *Try this for the hands*, she said. *It'll take away any stain we know. But my mother used to say that to cleanse the soul you need to wash in someone's tears.*

I thought we had done that already, Sybil said.

On some Sunday nights after Alf's shade whispered to her in the butcher's shop Sybil did not go to bed, but walked at the edge of the salt lake. At other times she telephoned Gawain Evans, who was always delighted to go to Sybil's home and bed – he being a gentle man who rather enjoyed being controlled by Sybil's strength and anger. These Sunday nights fuelled his addiction to Sybil, and he would beg her

186

to let him stay, to let him live there with her. But this was not a thing Sybil would discuss, and her flat *No* became a full stop to the night.

On the Sunday after she had seen the photos from the camera in Macha's kit-bag, Brigid Connor dressed for church as usual. Granna, also as usual for a Sunday morning, sat on the old couch on the verandah, with a cup of tea and two pieces of buttered toast.

Sure you're not coming? Brigid said to Granna.

Now why would I change a habit I like? Granna said. *And I wouldn't be asking Macha either. She'll not be putting on clothes for anyone.*

And why not? Brigid said briskly. *She's always come to church with me. Macha*, she called. *I'm ready.* When Macha didn't appear, Brigid knocked on her bedroom door. *Come on, Macha, we'll be late.*

But when Brigid opened the door the room was empty – no Macha, no rifle, no sign of Macha dressing to attend church.

She left early, Granna said. And indeed Macha was at that moment at her shelter in the Yackoo, sitting by a small fire and with no apparent interest in going anywhere.

Brigid sat next to Granna on the couch. *I don't understand all this*, she said. *I wish I could know what's going on in her head. I'd rather have all the pain myself than see Mach go through this. I feel so bloody helpless.* She picked up Granna's cup and took a long drink of tea. *And surely the things she's seen would make her turn to the church for peace, if nothing else.*

Granna snorted. *It seems to me,* she said, *it really seems to me, Brigid, that it's exactly the things she's seen that's making her not want anything to do with a two-faced god who seems to support both sides.*

Brigid gazed out across the paddocks of the Two Mile, towards the Yackoo where she thought Macha would be. *Do you remember when she was six or so?* she said. *She loved coming to church. There she'd be, this little thing with such a big voice, singing away – but not the hymns, she didn't know the words of the hymns. 'Baa-baa Black Sheep' was the favourite, I think, and 'Twinkle Twinkle Little Star'. No matter what the tune was that the rest of us sung, Mach sang her own song.*

So, no matter how often Brigid raised the subject over the dinner table during the week, come Sunday morning Macha was not there waiting to attend church with her mother. Instead she disappeared into the bush or walked towards the inland, for these were places full of silence, and where Macha was most at home.

CHAPTER NINE
HARVEST HOME

There are intensities in a life of an individual or of a place that gather and swirl around each other like a whirlpool. Those involved look for reasons, for the one thing that these events gather around. But there is no one thing, just a gathering and heaping, like black thunderheads looming on the horizon.

GRANNA, WHEN SHE TOLD THE STORY OF THIS DAY, always started it: *Now, Siggy Butow may have been a bit strange, but he was nothing if not courageous.*

Young George Aberline was a good man, a hard worker, and well aware of his responsibilities to his family and of God to him, and so when his business of salt-mining showed no signs of leaping to the heights of production that he expected, Young George asked the Reverend Siggy Butow to bless the venture. He said to David, *Maybe He can beat the bank to the business, because if He doesn't I think we're going to be up the bloody creek without a bloody paddle.* He gave a snorted laugh. *Or maybe it's out in the middle of the salt lake without a pot to piss in!*

So there they were, the ladies of the Church Auxiliary and the men of the Harvest Festival Committee. They sat with egg sandwiches and cups of tea in hand, peacefully anticipating agreement on the usual details of the Harvest Festival service, when up booms Young George Aberline:

Why don't we hold it at the lake, Siggy? Then you can do a combined service – you can help the salt harvest with a blessing, and celebrate the Harvest Festival out there in the paddocks where it all happens.

The chorus of agreement to this suggestion made Young George glow. It also made it impossible for Siggy Butow to disagree without exposing his fear of the open expanses that lay beyond the comparative safety of the town, for he had told no-one of his first and only venture to the top of the rock just after he had arrived.

In that case, Siggy said through his sandwich, *it must be an early service.* No-one questioned why this was so. *And of course we can't take the organ, or a piano, so you – we – must sing acapella. That means without music.* He paused, and Gloria Aberline and Martha Hinks later agreed that there was a slight waspishness in his voice as he said, *You do realise that your – our – singing may sound a little thin out there, in all that space. As long as you don't mind, of course.* Siggy drained his teacup and put it down, quite firmly, on the trestle table. *And will those arranging for the usual offerings of the Harvest Festival please find a suitable place at the lake edge, and convey the information to me?*

So it happened that very early on a mild spring morning – for Siggy Butow followed the calendar of the European festivals, allowing no reversal for the Antipodes – the Ladies Auxiliary of the Methodist congregation of Siddon Rock and their husbands gathered at the edge of the perpetual pool of the salt lake. With them came a truckload of baled hay. The men heaved some of the bales into rows as makeshift pews, and two pushed together as a base with another on top made a creditable, if unstable, pulpit. It was, however, the design and construction of hay bale display shelves that excelled. With Martha Hinks as overseer, this was done simply and to great effect: the back row was three bales long and three bales high, held in place by a tall stake hammered into the ground behind each bale, and with another at each side end. In front of this was placed a second row two bales high, and the front shelf was a simple one-bale row, staked in the front for stability.

The shelves were a huge success, and the ladies were hurrying now to arrange the Harvest Festival offerings, expecting Reverend Butow to appear at any moment. Baskets of goods were unloaded from the cars and trucks. On the top shelf jars of last summer's bottled fruit were stacked into pyramids, incandescent as the early morning sunlight shone through the purple of plums and yellows of peaches and apricots. *Could be a stained-glass window*, Gloria Aberline commented, *specially with these flowers in front of them*. Gloria was arranging big bunches of the pink everlastings that grew wild in early spring, and they did indeed make a delightful picture against the colours of the bottled fruit.

The second shelf was dedicated to several baskets of eggs, packed in straw for protection. The spaces between these were also filled with everlastings. *Why DOES Mister Butow have our festival in spring?* Mrs Sinclair Johnson said crossly. *It should be in autumn, and we'd have so much more to put out. Instead it all looks so . . . so thin.* Murmured agreement came from the other women.

Mister Placer, the station-master, dragged a large sack from the back of his car. *Grew these in that sheltered patch behind the railway station last year*, he said. *And they keep so well. If I put them along here they'll fill in and give more colour.* And the piles of mixed pumpkins did indeed look superb on the bottom shelf. The pale grey-green of three Queensland Blues contrasted nicely with the orangey-red colour of several other unusual-looking pumpkins. *No*, Mary Placer said to a query, *we don't know what those funny-looking ones are. They just appeared in the garden. They're different when they're cooked too. Quite a different texture to the Blue. I don't really like it m'self.*

Young George Aberline brought a lamb, as he did every year. Usually the beast would be tethered in the churchyard, waiting to go with the other offerings to the hospital kitchen. Siggy, at the first Harvest Festival after his arrival, made a small joke about the bleating lamb in the yard, calling it *the Lamb of God*, not realising that it was bound for the plates of hospital patients and staff. This year Young George tied it to a bale, but with enough slack rope for the beast to enjoy a salt lick from the dried salt at the edge of the lake.

On the hay bale pews, members of the congregation arranged themselves in their usual pattern, with various Aberlines taking the three rows on the left-hand side of the aisle, and the Sinclair Johnson and Abe Simmons families and other individuals almost filling the right-hand side. Miss Pearson, the organist, sat uneasily in the front row, unfamiliar without the masking bulk of the church organ. There they sat in the sharp clarity of early morning, waiting for Siggy Butow.

Siggy had told Sinclair Johnson, when interviewed for the 'Welcome to Siddon Rock' article, that he had climbed in the French Alps and that *there's nothing like a good climb up the mountains to make a man feel like a god.* Today he took a deep breath before stepping out the door and, he thought, handled the walk to the base of the silo well.

He stood there looking at the narrow track winding up the rock where he had climbed that one time, and remembered vividly the nausea in his gut when he had reached the top and seen the vast openness that he knew continued beyond the horizon. At Siggy's left another, broader track led around the base of the rock. He stepped towards this, then hesitated. If his parishioners could see the indecision: the high road or the low road? The shorter track up the rock, or the flat, longer, but easier walk around its side? Siggy was alone, there was no-one to see his dilemma. Better to walk around than climb up and try to conduct the service with a bellyful of collywobbles. But to conquer the fear, surely this was the thing? Not this time, old chap; this time the test was just to get there.

Siggy Butow followed the track around the edge of the rock: across the narrow margin between the rock and the cemetery, through a section of open ground and into a small patch of low-growing mallee. These were nothing like any trees he had seen in England or Europe, or even during his short stay in the capital on his way to Siddon Rock. These trees had several trunks growing from a base – thin, whippy red wood that looked as if it would never break. He walked past Nell's hut, not seeing it in his absorption with the trees; but he did notice some strange-looking dogs lying in the shade, and walked on somewhat faster and more purposefully.

As Siggy reached open ground again, he could hear his congregation talking although he could not see them yet. He heard Young George Aberline say, *I'm going to contact those blasted Bush Bashers again. Just look at that old machinery sitting there.*

Can't see them wanting them now anyway, Abe Simmons replied. *How many years ago was that? Four? Five? And just look at what the salt has done to them in such a short time. Can you imagine anyone wanting to use that tractor now, all rusted up and falling apart. They're real old dinosaurs.*

Yeah, Sinclair Johnson said. *Look at that huge old bulldozer standing there with its scoop up – come to think of it, it could be a Tyrannosaurus rex waiting to strike.*

The voices were clear, and he knew that around the next curve in the rock was the lack of containment that had frightened him off the rock and into reclusion at the Methodist manse. He peered around the curve and yes, there was his congregation huddled at the edge of the salt lake like a small flock of sheep. They looked lost under the vastness of the deep blue dome of sky that swept below all horizons. At Brigid Connor's fence several dun-coloured merino rams gathered, warily watching the unfamiliar intrusion.

Siggy pulled back. At that moment there was only himself, just the beating of his heart, the quivering breath in his lungs. Black threads floated across his eyes, and the swirling nausea began. But he was prepared this time; from his pocket he took a packet of peppermints, popped one in his mouth and leaned back against the rock for a few minutes until the nausea subsided somewhat. *It's all in knowing what to expect*, he thought. *I can handle this.*

And so Siggy Butow arrived at the Harvest Festival service at the salt lake. *How cheerful he looked when he arrived*, the chatter went later. *Full of confidence, he was. And didn't he tell us a story before the service, about what the hills and dales of his Yorkshire are like. You'd never have guessed. Just goes to show, you can't judge a book by its cover.*

After greeting his waiting flock, shaking hands and admiring the display behind them, Siggy placed himself behind the straw pulpit and smiled at the congregation. He felt in his jacket pocket for the book of services . . . and found it empty. The nausea swept back and his mind trembled precariously as he realised that his memory, not the best at any time, would not serve him well with two services to combine.

Siggy stood there dumbly, trying to decide what to do: postpone the service and go get the book? Cancel it altogether? Admit he'd forgotten the book and try to adlib?

197

Miss Pearson, knowing him as well as she did from anticipating his words every Sunday, was aware there was a problem and thought that he was waiting for the organ to play the introductory hymn. She stood suddenly and started to sing:

> *We plough the fields, and scatter*
> *The good seed on the land,*
> *But it is fed and watered*
> *By God's almighty hand . . .*

The congregation hesitated to its feet and joined in, the words drifting thinly across the treeless paddock between the lake and the rock.

> *He sends the snow in winter,*
> *The warmth to swell the grain,*
> *The breezes and the sunshine*
> *And soft, refreshing rain.*

By the end of the verse Siggy Butow's well-developed sense of ritual and theatre had exerted itself and, finding the hay bale pulpit too unstable to hold firmly at each side, he tucked one hand into his jacket and looked sternly at his parishioners, motioning them to be seated.

Was the sea of Galilee an inland lake, he roared suddenly, making the grazing rams start and run a few steps, *strong enough to take a man's weight?* His normal stance took over for a moment, and he raised his head.

Bright blue sky rushed down at him, and he quickly brought his gaze back to his congregation. Martha Hinks said later that she felt as if she had been singled out by those fierce eyes, and indeed she had started to rise to answer the question, when Siggy continued.

Today we celebrate the gifts of the harvest and this glorious and imposing lake of salt. This magnificent place on God's earth is like that which our Lord knew, with its lake and open spaces. He carefully kept his eyes off the horizon as he spoke. *Like those who lived at Galilee and fished its waters, here too will be an enterprise to make us proud. Young George Aberline and his son David will bring more prosperity to the town by their business of salt-mining.*

So bless, oh Lord, this enterprise of Geo. Aberline & Son Minerals. Let it prosper and use your gift for the good of all. And at the same time, bless our harvest of grain from these fertile paddocks.

Bloody fool, Young George muttered to Sinclair Johnson, *he doesn't even know that the effin' salt buggers up 'these fertile paddocks'.*

Without warning, Miss Pearson stood again.

Sowing in the morning, sowing seeds of kindness,
Sowing in the noontide and the dewy eve;
Waiting for the harvest, and the time of reaping,
We shall come rejoicing, bringing in the sheaves.

The startled congregation let Miss Pearson take the solo, but they rose as one to sing the rollicking chorus:

Bringing in the sheaves,
bringing in the sheaves,
We shall come rejoicing,
bringing in the sheaves . . .

There at the edge of the salt lake, with no walls to hold them back, the usual harmonies expanded as the Methodists found a new rhythm. They swung into the next verse and chorus with a gusto not heard in the confines of the small church building.

Sowing in the sunshine, sowing in the shadows,
Fearing neither clouds nor winter's chilling
  breeze;
By and by the harvest, and the labour ended,
We shall come rejoicing, bringing in the sheaves.

Bringing in the sheaves,
bringing in the sheaves,
We shall come rejoicing,
bringing in the sheaves.

As the last note flew away across the salt lake the unease in Siggy Butow's gut was becoming worse and he wondered if he could finish now. But the congregation settled expectantly onto their hay pews, glowing from the singing and waiting for the full Harvest Festival service they knew so well. Siggy concentrated his gaze inward as his gut churned threateningly. Straw rustled as movement of legs and bottoms on the bales signalled the need to begin. So Siggy started talking, feeling as though he were plucking words from the air itself.

As this day is such a special one, and since we began with a blessing on a new venture, we shall depart from the usual order of service. The straw bales stopped rustling as everyone settled to listen. *Man is but a steward of the earth,* he went on. *The earth and all its convolutions are made by God. This lake is made by God, and all the things in it. Should there be beasts beneath the water or on the land, these are made by God, for his own recognition, but we must remember his words in Revelations 14, Verse 11: 'They have no rest day or night, who worship the beast and his image, and whosoever receiveth the mark of his name.'* Here Siggy Butow paused, wondering how he had arrived at this, but the feeling of slight dizziness and disconnection with all around him pushed him on.

Our town is sheltered by the rock, but our town is regularly visited by great storms of dust. Siggy was speaking faster now, keeping his gaze firmly on the ground just in front of the hay bale pews. *But what is this dust? I'll tell you what it is. It's the whole world that preceded us, for each grain of dust can melt a glacier. Remnants of the dinosaurs have been ground down by time into minute particles* . . . Siggy paused, and his befuddled mind called up images of dinosaurs striding through the huge dust storm that had engulfed the town on the night Macha Connor came home.

On the front hay bale Miss Pearson began to rise, as did the confused members of the church, who were watching her for cues as to what was expected of them. They sat again as Siggy continued.

The dust of the galaxies is also there, in the dust storms. Each time the town has a dust storm, we are covered with stardust. Ashes to ashes, dust to dust . . . but the dust never goes away. We wear the world – the galaxy – on our shoulders and in our lungs . . . and the Lord said, 'Dust thou art, and unto dust shalt thou return.'

As he spoke these last words, Siggy Butow looked up and there, in the open paddock between the lake and an impenetrable-looking line of bush, was a group of dinosaurs. They were not green as he would have expected, but dark brown with patches of faded yellow and silvery white. There they stood, immobile and menacing.

The shuffling sounds of the uneasy congregation faded, and an ancient timbre filled his head. Siggy heard a bleating scream that could have been from a gigantic prehistoric sheep, and there was an enormous thundering roar from the dinosaurs. Underneath this cacophony a cracking noise came from the lake, sounding as if the world was being split apart. This last was too much for Siggy's distressed mind and gut. He turned and vomited behind the straw pulpit, then rushed up the path over the rock to the confining safety of the Methodist manse.

The next Sunday at the after-service supper Siggy apologised to his bewildered congregation, citing an upset stomach as the reason for his abrupt departure. He sent out tentative feelers in conversation to see if anyone else had heard the roaring and cracking noises that had been the last straw for his strength of will. It appeared that he had been the only one. What he did hear, however, was concern at the quality of the sermon. *A bit confusing*, Young George said. And *I didn't really understand all that stuff about dinosaurs and stardust, Mr Butow*, came from Gloria Aberline. For the next several Sundays the Methodist sermons were stern and straightforward, upholding the biblical text as written as the only truth to be held to.

For a while there was discussion in the pub and around the town as to whether the Reverend Butow had seen a beast of some sort in the salt lake. *After all, who knows what's in there or how long it's been there?* But Young George Aberline stilled the speculation. *There's nothing about a salt lake in the early records*, he said. *Old Henry Aberline's diary specifically says how dry the place was. No mention of the lake at all. And you DO know what's under the bloody water, at least around the edges. A friggin' lot of our farms.* But Young George also thought, and kept to himself, *who would know what could have happened beneath the enigmatic, mirror-like surface of the lake.*

Siggy Butow, as he rushed up the rock in his blind panic to get back to the safety of the manse, had not seen three women watching the service from the top of the rock.

Macha, after her final round of the town just after dawn, had made her way over the rock on her way to the

Yackoo where she stayed most mornings before going to the Two Mile at lunch-time. She stopped at the top when she saw the unaccustomed activity at the lake-edge.

As Macha stood watching, Nell, drawn by the unusual early morning sounds of vehicles on the sandy and pitted track to the lake, climbed the north face of the rock from her hut. She walked up to Macha and put her arm around her. Catalin, on her early morning walk, hesitated when she arrived a few minutes later, not wanting to intrude into what appeared to be a private moment of communion.

Nell waved Catalin forward. *This's Macha*, she said to Catalin. *She got things she can't say, too.*

Macha pulled back, prepared to run from the ghosts surrounding Catalin. But Nell's arm made it difficult to pull away. Catalin put out her hand, and then looked closely at Macha's face. There she saw an old and familiar message, one she had not expected in this country so far from the European war. *Too much death*, it said, *too much horror.* She changed her gesture from a handshake to something closer and warmer, taking both Macha's hands in hers. *I know*, she said, and she could have been speaking to either Macha or Nell. *I know.*

Macha's expression did not change, but she held Catalin's hands for a long moment. The ghosts, it seemed, were not to do with her but were Catalin's alone.

Nell, Catalin and Macha watched the Harvest Festival service, the singing thin but clear in the crystalline air of the inland morning. Catalin smiled when Nell added her own rhythm to 'Bringing in the Sheaves' but Macha seemed not to notice. When Siggy Butow rushed up the rock the women stepped out of the way so he could pass, and were not concerned that he offered no greeting; indeed, did not seem to see them at all.

From then on Macha was often at the hospital grounds at the time of Catalin's afternoon break. This happened when Jos was at school, so Catalin and Macha would walk up the rock or out to the lake. They needed no words to be comfortable together.

As for the salt-mining business of Young George Aberline, even though it was blessed by the church the manager at the State and Farmers' Bank said that he wanted to see a financial report. And that would have to be immediately.

After their visit to Brittany, Young George and David had taken up the methods of the French salt-miners. These well suited them, as no machinery or structures were needed, just time to build pond areas, and the special rakes imported from France. It was this very lack of infrastructure that had made the manager at the State and Farmers' Bank place a mortgage over Young George's farm when funding the venture.

Geo. Aberline & Son Minerals may have given work to several young men in the town, but the company had failed to produce a single salt-cellar of usable salt. It was not that Young George and David did not try. Producers of salted fish or meat, or even of salt-licks for cattle and sheep, were simply not interested in the strangely coloured and bitter salt of Siddon Rock. Young George and David sought out trappers and animal hide preservers, but no sales eventuated when a cloudy yellow film appeared on all hides and furs treated with the mineral. Even potteries, when given samples of the salt to test in glazes, declined to buy. The Capital Commercial Pottery said no matter what type of glaze they used, a yellow overglaze changed the original colour. This was particularly grotesque when their popular blue glaze emerged from the kiln as a sickly acid-green.

Young George sat up for several nights worrying about his salt, and finally sent a sample to laboratories in the capital. He thought that if the contamination could be identified they could find a way of cleaning the salt. When the report came back it merely stated that there was an *unidentified contaminant of unknown origin*. At the bottom of the typed page was a handwritten note: *The composition of this sample is unusual. Under the microscope the crystals are strangely shaped and connected in a manner I've not seen before. Can you send me more samples for analysis?* And it was signed *Jordan Hatherley, Chief Scientist, Research Section*.

Young George took a sample of the salt to Doctor Allen and asked if he could have a look at it under his microscope, saying, *If I can't work out what's going on, Doc, there won't be a salt-works business left*. The men took turns in looking, but the oblongated crystals told them nothing of their strangeness.

Sybil Barber heard of the problem from Brigid Connor as she collected the bread and meat for the Two Mile. *Tell Young George to bring some in*, Sybil said. *I'll try it in the bread and corned beef.* To Sybil's dismay, when she took the bread from the oven it had formed a flat, lumpen stodge with a strange yellow pattern through the dough.

The corned beef fared even worse, but luckily Sybil was warned by the bread disaster and tried only one piece. When she took it from the brine she telephoned Young George to come to the shop.

Now Sybil was renowned for her corned beef, and she guarded its method carefully. She had found the handwritten recipe during her renovations of Barber's Butchery & Bakery, under the ancient linoleum and layers of newspaper that acted as lining. *Irish Spiced Beef.* When she read the recipe Sybil realised this certainly wasn't something that Alf Barber had done. Later, she set about the time-consuming spicing and cooking, and turned local beef into something similar to the ancient Irish delicacy. Now, with a tweak of difference here and there, Irish Spiced Beef had become known for miles around as well worth the trip to Siddon Rock.

It was, then, understandable that Sybil was considerably upset by the appearance of a particularly nasty and nauseating yellow-green film on the beef. It was this she telephoned Young George to come and see. Together they considered what combination of minerals could have caused this, until Sybil lost patience and sent a perturbed Young George off with, as she told Granna, *a flea in his ear.*

Granna wrinkled her nose at the foul-looking meat lying in the tray. *Good grief, I wouldn't feed that to the dogs*, she said. *But you've got to feel sorry for the man; that salt's been lying fallow for generations. The concentration of George Henry must be enormous.*

What do you mean? Sybil had no knowledge of George Henry's story.

It was George Henry who started the salt lakes, on his journey into the desert. Granna always liked telling this story. *Just look at the map of salt lakes from here towards the inland and you'll see where he peed – and other things.* Some details were too personal for even Granna to elaborate on. *Salt drawn up from the earth mingling with the salt of his body fluids, that's what started them all. And our own lake is even worse, because that's where he drowned himself too, so it's concentrated George Henry in the dry salt.*

That's disgusting. Sybil took the water she had used for the experimental corned beef and poured it down the sink. *So why did he drown himself anyway?*

Something to do with business, I think. Granna was purposely vague. *I don't rightly remember. But things done way back do have a way of showing up later.* And with that, she left the shop.

At the State and Farmers' Bank, Young George and David gave the manager the report on the salt-mining business. As he read it he pursed his lips and drummed his fingers on the desk next to the single page of handwritten notes. Then he smoothed a hand over his already slick hair and said, *The debt must be cleared. Immediately. There is no indication in here that this business will ever be anything but bad. Where, may I ask, has the money gone?*

I don't know, Young George said. *I don't understand it at all.*

Obviously not into the business. The manager was less than sympathetic.

But where else? Young George was perplexed and more than a little distressed. *It's not as if there's been a lot of payments. All we've had are wages, and they're not much, and some payments for formwork for the ponds, and the rakes. Then bags, of course, for the finished salt. That's all there, stored in the shed on the farm. And some costs for when I travel around trying to get someone to buy it. Not much at all really, certainly not a whole farm's worth.*

I told you last time that it had to be showing a profit, the manager said.

No. Young George was adamant, and his practical self took over. *Something's wrong. At least let me have a real look at the accounts before you sell everything out from under me.*

The manager steepled his fingers and leaned over the wide desk towards Young George. *Two days*, he said. *Two days and not a minute more.*

And so Young George and David sat down with the box of paper that made up their accounting records and sorted the bills into one pile and the payments into another. And indeed there were not many papers in either pile.

David added up the bills pile, and Young George added up the payments. They did not equal each other, with the payments considerably more than the bills.

Forgot the wages, David said, and added them to the bills list, but this made little difference. There was still a huge gap, even when they swapped piles and recalculated.

Give me the chequebook, Young George said, and on every payment that had been made he wrote a cheque number.

This is too messy, David said. *Let's do it right.* And he ruled up a piece of paper with three columns: Bills, Payments, Cheque number/Cash payment. An hour later all columns were filled with matching figures: Bill: £25, Payment: £25, Cheque number: 1. Every bill, payment and cheque that had been paid was recorded in three columns, from the day they started building the first channel to the last wages cheque. Just a few lines were needed for expenditures, and a couple of pages for wages, for Young George had been correct when he had told the bank manager that there had been few expenses.

Now, David said, *every row across is correct. So when we add up the columns down, there's no reason that they won't all be equal.* But when he finished, equal they most certainly were not.

Then Young George tried, adding each column three times and getting three lots of different answers. *This is ridiculous*, he said, and thought of Brigid Connor doing his sums at school for him. *I'm going to get Brigid, she's the smart one.*

Brigid Connor arrived the next morning with a box of old farm papers that she'd found when clearing out her own office at the Two Mile. *Brought these for you to look through while I'm sorting out your mess,* she said cheerfully. *They're really old records. If you're interested, right at the bottom of the box is George Henry's stuff from the first stock and station agency.*

Brigid checked every entry in every column in the ledger of Geo. Aberline & Son Minerals. She added them across and down, and still they would not correlate. She went to the verandah where Young George sat staring out at his land and David was reading old records from the box she had brought.

Well, I'm damned if I know what's going on. Brigid was puzzled. *No matter what I do, these bloody figures have a life of their own. They just don't want to be the same as each other. I think you have to take them to the bank and see what they can make of them. I'm sure they can sort it out.*

David held up an old ledger he had been looking through. *Well, whatever the problem is, our book-keeping can't be any worse than George Henry's. He'd have to have been the worst businessman ever. Look, there's absolutely nothing in this ledger, except for one entry. See here,* he held up the dusty book, *all it says is 'Debt repaid'. And look at the signature. It's not G. H. Aberline, like all the other old papers. It looks like Beally, or Beatty, or . . .*

I don't give a rat's arse for that old stuff, Young George snapped. Through the night, the *thunk* of an auctioneer's hammer closing the sale of his farm had kept him awake, and this morning it was a regular beat in his head. *Bloody well concentrate on sorting this lot out because if we don't the farm goes and we end up with bloody nothing.*

But sorting it out was not possible and they went again to the bank. There the manager looked at the figures that did not correlate, looked at the debt to be paid, looked at the lack of assets in Geo. Aberline & Son Minerals. His face became shut and stony.

Look here, David said, and put the report about the unusual crystals in front of the manager, turning it to face him so that he could read it without exertion.

Yes, Young George said eagerly. *Look. This could be the making of the town. Something different is happening in the salt at the lake. We'll find out what it is, and make it work for us.*

But the Aberlines had to admit that they had not yet sent off more samples, and that there was no income from the business, yet a lot of money had been spent on it.

All I know, the manager said, *is that your accounts are in chaos and can't be understood by anyone. The business is obviously unviable. The debt has to be paid back, and paid back now. Can you do that?*

Young George recognised the churning in his gut as despair. He shook his head. David looked out the window towards the wild seas of the English Channel.

In that case the auction will be next month, to give us time to advertise both the farm and the business. If things change in the meantime, please come in immediately.

The town rallied around for the Aberline mortgagee sale, but the debt was too large to be redeemed by friends and neighbours buying this and that and returning them to Young George. The farm itself was sold to Fatman Aberline, who was finding that his acreage wasn't producing as much as it used to, and needed more land.

Sorry, Young George, he said to his uncle. *But better me than some stranger who doesn't know the place.*

As for the business of Geo. Aberline & Son Minerals, no-one thought it worth bidding on, and within twelve months the channels and crystallising pans disappeared back into the smooth glitter of the lake.

Young George, that man who thought he had escaped the sadness of the Aberlines, saw his son onto the train to the capital. There David found work on a passenger ship as a steward, and returned to the coast of Brittany where his experience as a salt-worker gave him residency. *I feel right at home here*, he wrote in his letters to Young George. *It's so flat and salty, if you remember the landscape. And I don't have to squint very much to see the lighthouse offshore as our silo.*

As for Young George himself, the man who was de facto mayor of Siddon Rock disappeared from the town's view, going to neither church nor the pub but staying put in Brigid Connor's married couple's cottage at the Two Mile, where he moved with his self-effacing wife, Hettie. He helped Brigid on the farm, and at night he sat on the front step of the cottage and pondered the strange convolutions of life. He found himself thinking about his grandfather, George Henry Aberline, and wondered if this was how he had felt before he drowned himself in the salt lake. Sometimes Macha sat with him for a few minutes, for even though she said nothing, she knew well enough how the language of a place can suddenly change and not be understood.

CHAPTER TEN

THERE ARE ALWAYS HOLES IN THE FABRIC

Knit one, purl one, pass the slipstitch over.

THE SPRING BALL was the annual peak of social activity in the district, and the year Young George Aberline's farm was sold by the bank was no exception.

For Alistair Meakins, the only source of gowns in the district, there were moments during the weeks before the first Saturday of September when he wished he was in any other trade, in any other town except Siddon Rock. But the women of the town and outlying farms relied on his immaculate judgement, and knew him as friend and confidant. They were at ease discussing different styles of gowns. They took notice when Alistair quoted the *Berlei Review*, emphasising how important well-fitting undergarments were to the hang of a skirt or the smoothness of a bodice. At this time of the year Alistair's expertise was stretched to its limit as he advised and assisted each woman, always aware that duplication of any sort would not be tolerated.

Each year Alistair prepared for the onslaught of customers demanding original gowns by bringing in consignments on approval from several suppliers, so that the unwanted ones could be returned. For weeks he advised on gown style and colours, suggesting a soft flowing fabric to some and steering others towards more concealing brocades and satins. Brigid Connor, for instance, who was thin and wiry from years of physical work, looked wonderfully feminine in an ornate bodice and flowing skirt; whereas a firmly woven fabric helped Marge Redall hold her more generous qualities in check.

This year Marge chose a gown of lustre satin, and Alistair quipped that her cloud of blue notes would look quite stunning against the deep amethyst colour. As he pinned and marked where to ease the fit a little across the hips, Alistair glanced up at the Dior poster on the wall of the fitting room and was not surprised to catch a look of puzzled bemusement in the model's eyes. *Don't you look like that*, he thought wryly, *not all of us are tall and skinny. We just have to do the best with what we have.*

Marge was also looking at the poster of the elegant Dior model posed against a backdrop of the Eiffel Tower. *Penny for your thoughts, Marge*, Alistair said.

I went to Paris once, Marge replied. *Before I met Bluey it was. Years before the war. There's a bridge there that was built in 1578. We can't imagine that here, can we. To walk on something built nearly four hundred years ago.*

Alistair sat back and looked closely at Marge. There was something in her voice that was an ill-fit with her tough appearance, a musicality when she spoke of Paris. *Well, aren't you the dark horse*, he said. *You've not said anything before about being in Europe.*

There are things we don't spout around, aren't there? Marge said. *Years ago. A different place, a different life.* Marge was quiet then until Alistair finished marking alterations and she left the shop.

Some nights during these weeks before the ball, after he had expended what he thought was his last iota of energy, Alistair went home and collapsed on the chair on his verandah. He was quite unable to think of food, let alone cook for himself. *But at least*, he thought, *it's nothing like the time during the war.*

As the war in Europe had spread and sucked the world into its vortex, Alistair mourned the loss of style. The goods displayed to him by travelling salesmen became skimpier and shoddier, and he told the anxious salesmen that *to look at them almost breaks my heart.*

Skirts lost their swirl, sewing thread broke and materials thinned until they disappeared. But it was the lack of underwear that particularly concerned Alistair. He wrote letters to new suppliers and spent a fortune on telephone calls, all to no effect. No matter where he tried, a decent brassiere or an elegant pair of knickers was not to be found.

This last indignity put him on the train to the capital in search of a solution, but after two long days of visiting manufacturers he had found nothing but empty warehouses and silent machinery.

At the U-form Lingerie Factory a sign nailed to the open front door proclaimed an Auction Sale of Goods and Equipment to be held the following week. Alistair walked around the factory floor through the rows of silent sewing machines, considering the degree of difficulty in their use. He sat at one, thinking through the workings of the mechanism. When he was convinced he could use it he went straight to the auctioneer's office. Within a few minutes he owned a commercial machine, several bolts of fine linen and assorted lengths of underwear silk and celanese in peach, pink and ecru. In the boxes were also matching sewing thread, various widths of elasticised cotton, hook-and-eye fasteners, bundles of laces and trims, and a package containing paper patterns for slips, knickers and brassieres. He thought he was finished then, but the auctioneer drew him aside. *You might want to look at these*, he said.

Alistair opened a square of blue tissue paper, and shook out a length of black silk. It was so light and fine that it floated in the air like a dark pool. *I'll have this*, he said. *There's about enough for a set, and I know just the person to make it for.*

Then the auctioneer unrolled a length of watermark silk taffeta. Even in the dusty storeroom light the blue and green shimmered like the wings of a dragonfly.

That too, Alistair said. *All of it. It's too beautiful to leave behind.*

Alistair arranged to have his purchases delivered to his home by one of the travelling salesmen who visited him

220

regularly. He had no desire to have the town know that he had them.

When the goods arrived Alistair rearranged the lounge-room by placing one of the large chairs on the back verandah and throwing over it a brightly coloured cover that had been on the shelf of the shop for some time. The reds and yellows in the material gave the usually neat and prim verandah a rakish air. *Quite Spanish-looking,* Alistair thought. In the storage shed behind the shop there was a small table and, by balancing this on the trolley he used for moving boxes of goods, he dragged it down the lane to his house where it fitted perfectly into the space left by the chair.

Alistair spent two Sundays dismantling and re-assembling the sewing machine, with the assistance of an old instruction book the auctioneer had given him. When he had the machine running smoothly, he unfolded the paper patterns and set out to discover the workings of women's underwear.

Alistair started with a petticoat. He studied the shape of each pattern piece, comparing it with a garment taken from the shop. *Brilliantly done,* he murmured, when he saw how folding and sewing material into darts moulded the garment to the shape of the body.

After several evenings of study he decided that the patterns were only a guide to proportion and the best angle to cut the material for maximum effect; and, with the assistance of a set of *Women's Mirror Sewing Guides* to tell him about finishing and detailing, he tested his skill with a piece of the cheapest material. To his delight the petticoat formed easily under his hands. *Can't tell the difference*, he said as he compared the made garment with the one from the shop.

With confidence now he cut and sewed the first garments of a line of brassieres, panties and petticoats that he labelled *La'Mour Ladies Wear.* These he folded ready to take to the shop. The fine black silk he sewed into panties, camisole and a half-slip. He put this special and delicate lingerie in a tissue-lined box and placed it under the counter at the shop with a card attached – *for Allison.*

Now, with the war a recent memory and quality clothing, both under and upper, more easily available, Alistair considered ending the *La'Mour* range. It had become an albatross around his neck, as the garments were so popular that he spent all his free time cutting and sewing. He had, after Allison's walk down Wickton Street when she had seen Paris, thought about employing someone to sew for him. *After all*, he thought, *the great couturiers don't actually do the sewing themselves, do they.* But on consideration it did not seem to be a good idea, letting the town know that he made the range. *Things need to be from somewhere else to sell well*, he told himself. *It's not the same if things are local, not the same cachet.*

And so Alistair reluctantly continued to make the popular range of underwear in his lounge-room. But his heart was not in it, and he gradually stopped renewing out-of-stock pieces until the range ended by attrition.

If a customer complained about the disappearance of a favourite item he just said, *Everything changes, my dear. Maybe the firm's going out of business, but I'm sure I can find something equally as good, next time a travelling salesman comes through.*

The Monday before the Spring Ball Catalin stopped to chat with Alistair outside the shop, and he asked if she was going to the ball.

No, Catalin said.

Alistair was not put off by the brusque reply. *But if you did go, what would you wear?* he pressed.

Catalin shrugged. *It does not matter, because I do not go.*

Alistair knew that Catalin's wardrobe did not hold a gown suitable for a Spring Ball. But he, Alistair Meakins, would rise to the challenge. Did he not make a successful line of lingerie for the town? Had he not designed a hat made by the French hat-makers, Etablissements Werlé, Créateur de chapeaux féminins? And had not Allison walked the Avenue Montaigne in that selfsame hat, and gazed into the window of the House of Dior?

Alistair wanted to make Catalin a gown. Alistair was determined to make Catalin a gown. *This place needs a good dose of glamour*, Alistair said to himself as he walked home that evening. *And some of those would-be-if-they-could-be women who look down their noses at Catalin need a good shaking up. So let's do it right.*

That night Alistair took the length of silk taffeta that he had bought during the war and measured it by holding it lengthways from left shoulder to right fingertip. *About twelve yards. That should do nicely.*

Alistair caught sight of himself in the mirror with the fabric heaped at his feet and laughed. *I look like Venus being born*, he said to the image. He held the rustling taffeta tight at his waist, and the idea of the gown formed as he draped the material this way and that. *Yes*, he said, *yes. The new ballerina style – mid-calf length and as much fabric in the skirt as possible, with a tight bodice. Elegant and seductive. What more could a girl ask for? Now to work out her size.*

Alistair walked down the back lane to the shop. There in the fitting room he stood next to an unclothed plaster model, comparing his body with hers. A memory hovered, of Macha's tall, thin body marching into town, but Alistair ignored it and imagined the shape of Catalin. He knew that she was the same height as himself, and estimated that in size she was somewhere between himself and the thin model. *I can deal with that*, he said, and took the model home with him. His eye, so trained to the vagaries of the female form, guided him as he glued and moulded padding around the bust and hips, until the size and shape was, he thought, close to Catalin's.

The waist measurement seemed just about right, *but I'll worry about the length when it's made. I'm pretty sure that the shoulder to waist length is close, though. I think she's only a bit short from hip to knee, and that doesn't matter with a full skirt.*

Alistair started work that night, swiftly measuring, cutting and tacking pieces together with a loose stitch, so that by the early morning he had the beginnings of a ballerina-style gown. He stood back and looked at it critically, envisioning Catalin in the wide-cut neckline and tight-fitting bodice above a full, gathered skirt. The picture made him smile. Then he thought about how to entice Catalin to try on the garment and finally, reluctantly, decided that the only way was to ask her to his home, his sanctuary into which no-one in the town had set foot.

The next day he called to Catalin as she passed the shop. *Why don't you bring Jos to tea tonight?* he said. *Nothing fancy, just a different place for you to be for an hour or so.*

Alistair dragged the kitchen table into the lounge-room and set it with white linen and fragile-looking bone china. In the centre he placed a small vase of pale pink everlasting daisies. As a last touch he folded darker pink damask napkins through silver holders and put them next to each plate.

The spring evening was cool, so Alistair set kindling and paper in the fireplace ready to be lit. Then he arranged the model with the partly completed gown against the cream of the window curtains and angled a tall lamp so that it stood in a pool of light.

And how was school today, young Jos? Alistair called from the kitchen as he carved a leg of lamb into slices. *Getting on all right with the young ruffians, I hope.*

Catalin had noticed how intense Alistair's violet colour was when they arrived, and did not want to dim the sheen with careless words.

Jos does not speak to anyone but me, and he has just started to do this, she said gently. *Do not be offended, it's just how he is. And yes, he does well at school. Mr Best is very good with him.*

No offence at all, Alistair said. *We all have our ways of dealing with things, and it must have been a rough start in life for the kid. Now take Brigid Connor for instance. She seems all tough blokey talk and prickly reactions. But underneath she's as feminine as you are.*

Catalin laughed. *As me? But I am not feminine. Look at me, sitting here in trousers. I'm not a pink and pretty person at all.*

Pink and pretty isn't necessarily feminine, Alistair said from the kitchen. *I do hope you like lamb. It's all Sybil had left by the time I got there.*

Of course. We eat all meat, after not having any for so long. So what is feminine for you, Alistair?

Alistair brought out the platter of roast lamb and vegetables and put it down in front of Jos. *There you are, young fellow. You take as much as you like.* He turned to Catalin. *For me feminine is the essence,* he said thoughtfully. *It's the strength and desire under whatever surface the world sees, hidden away right at the heart of being.*

And sometimes masculine is hidden by the feminine, and sometimes the other way round, Catalin said quietly. *Sometimes nothing is really as it seems, is it.*

Alistair hesitated, feeling Allison wanting to speak with this immigrant woman.

Catalin continued. *Sometimes the surface cracks a little. Yes? And maybe someone who knows about surface and heart of being sees a little and understands.*

Allison begged to be let out. *She knows*, she said to Alistair, *I want to talk to her.* But Alistair just smiled brightly. *Of course, for every woman it's a bit different*, he said. *Take that dress there . . .*

Catalin laughed. *This glorious gown? But this is the soul of feminine.*

So say you, Alistair continued, making up the story as he spoke. *But the person I was making it for didn't think so. She wanted pink and pretty! Then she decided not to go to the ball at all. And so there it is, left hanging on that poor old plaster girl.*

Catalin got up and looked closer at the gown. *But Alistair, this is superb. The fabric, so beautiful. It too hides what it is. See how the colours change from blue to green. And there's a silvery sheen. It looks like the salt lake when the wind is blowing over it.* She moved the skirt under the light so that the surface rippled like small waves. *See, there is concealed colour. And such a beautiful cut it is. Where did you learn to do this?*

Alistair shrugged, pleased. *Just learnt as I went along, really. And I've seen . . . things. Things that taught me. I'd like to set up my own couture, but this isn't really the place for it, is it now?* He laughed. *Can you imagine? Alistair of Siddon Rock doesn't quite have the right ring about it, does it?*

Catalin returned to the table and helped herself to the lamb and vegetables. *But everywhere is exotic to someplace else. Europe is exotic to here. Here is exotic to Europe. Mundane is always where you are. Exotic is always where you are not. So, why not Alistair of Siddon Rock, selling in Europe?*

Why not indeed? Alistair said lightly. *It's a shame you don't want to go to the ball though. Here Jos, don't let this lamb go to waste. Have some more.* He pushed the plate in front of Jos and Catalin. *You too Cat, I hate waste. Anyway, I think this dress would come close to being your size, and I could finish it off for you to wear.*

Catalin waved away the plate. *Thank you, but I have eaten enough. And I could not do that, take the dress. I cannot owe you.*

Rubbish. If you don't, I'll have a half-finished gown on my hands forever. It would be such a waste of lovely fabric. Here, let me pour you a brandy while you think about it. Alistair turned to Jos. *What do you think, Jos? Would this gown look wonderful on your mother?*

Jos slid off the chair and went to the gown. He stroked the material of the skirt and turned, smiling at Catalin. *Mama,* he said. And the strangeness of the word from the silent child took Alistair's breath away. *Mama.*

Ah, Catalin said. *You think I should try it?*

Jos nodded. Catalin turned to Alistair. *So, do you think I should take the opinion of a six-year-old boy?*

Alistair laughed. *I think you should definitely take the opinion of this one. He seems to have a natural eye for beauty.*

Catalin changed into the gown in Alistair's bedroom and walked back into the lounge-room where Alistair had lit the fire against the chill. *It fits perfectly*, she said. Alistair could hear the desire in the words.

Oh my, Alistair said. *Oh my. This is not the person we see walking around town. This is a very beautiful woman. The colour makes your hair and eyes look even darker. So dramatic.*

Catalin looked at herself in the mirror near the sewing machine, holding her wild hair at the nape of her neck. *I don't think I have ever had anything so delicious on my body*, she said. *I don't even look like me.*

This must be the inner you, Alistair said. *On display for the first time. You will let me finish it for you, won't you. It would be a sin not to.*

Yes. Catalin nodded. *Yes.*

She stood watching in the mirror as Alistair pinned the hem to the right length and made minor adjustments, smiling to himself as he did. *Pretty good guess for size, if I do say so myself*, he thought. *Quite magical, really.* When it was a perfect fit he put it back on the model, and moved it next to the sewing machine. *I'll have to let the skirt hang for a couple of days because it's cut on the cross of the material, you see. And if we don't let it hang, it'll drop unevenly later. So why don't you come back on Friday night, and we'll make certain it's right, and you can take it then.* He turned off the bright light overhead so that the room was lit only by the standard lamp and by firelight. *Now, another brandy before you take Jos home to bed?*

Thank you, Catalin said, *that would be lovely. Jos, come and sit by the fire.* Jos laughed, but was nowhere to be seen.

All right, young man, where are you?

Jos's laughter filled the room, but Catalin and Alistair could not tell where it came from. Then he crawled out from under the gown, sitting on the floor as the blue-green taffeta flowed off his head and shoulders like water.

Catalin picked up her son and hugged him. *You look wonderful in blue, or is it green*, she teased him. Then she turned to Alistair. *I still don't know, Alistair. I cannot go and leave Jos alone at night*, she said. *I could never do this.*

Leave him at the pub. Marge Redall won't go to the ball until late, and Bluey never goes. They love Jos and look after him like their own kid. You know that.

On the afternoon of the ball Catalin and Jos walked to the pub, Jos carrying a small bundle with his pyjamas and toothbrush wrapped in a towel.

It's just for tonight, Catalin said. *You go to bed and stay there asleep all night. And I'll come and get you as soon as I wake up tomorrow. All right?*

Jos smiled at his mother. *All right.*

Mrs Redall will give you your dinner tonight, you eat it all, even the bits you don't like. And then she will put you to bed. Mister Redall will be there all night, as he does not go to the ball. And he will come and see that you are asleep and happy. So, you go to bed, you just go to sleep, okay.

This is a safe place, good people. You know them. You'll be so safe.

Don't worry, Mama. Jos rubbed her arm. *You will come and get me in the morning.*

Of course, Jossie. Always I will come to get you. Catalin put her arm around her son and hugged him tightly. *Always. Look,* Catalin took a small torch from her bag. *Look. Put this under your pillow, and then if you get frightened by something, you can switch it on and shine it around the room. Then you will see there is nothing to be frightened by.*

And so it was that Jos had tea at the Railway and Traveller's Hotel on the night of the Spring Ball, and then went to sleep in a room off the first floor verandah, with the double doors propped open to let in the fresh night air. *Bluey's just down the stairs if you want anything*, Marge said. *You sleep well now.*

There she was, Catalin, in her room at the hospital, empty without Jos, filled with silence. In the high corners of the room murky green and grey colours flickered, but she was used to them hanging there and took no notice. The gown lay on her bed ironed and spread to avoid wrinkling the crisp taffeta. At the foot of the bed was a pile of folded tissue paper that Alistair had wrapped the gown in, and on the top piece Catalin wrote, in pencil: *To dance is to write poetry with the body. Tonight I dance the Australian way.*

She prepared herself carefully, mindful that this was her first appearance in the social stream of the town, and struggled to control her wild hair into a smooth and elegant chignon. She turned to the mirror, and in its tarnished glass saw her mother dressed in a floating sea-green gown that reflected the light of stars like echoes of ancient conflagrations. She laughed and touched the surface. *Viktoria Mama. I'm pleased to be you*, she said.

Catalin opened the cello case propped near her bed and took out the instrument. She ran her finger along its edge, seeking the words she knew so well:

> *Margit Catalin 1879 to 1930 ... Viktoria Margit ...*
> *Catalin Viktoria ... Josis Matthieu ...*

But her fingers told her the words had changed. Now they read:

> *Margit Catalin 1879 to 1930 ...Viktoria Margit 1899 to 1948 ...*
> *Catalin Viktoria ... Josis Matthieu ...*

And where the neck and body of the cello joined, there was a picture of Catalin's mother.

By seven o'clock on the night of the Spring Ball there was no sign that the social event of the year was about to begin.

Hidden at the rear of the hall, the Central Allstars unloaded their instruments from the covered truck and let themselves in through the stage door. The band, consisting of piano, fiddle, clarinet and drums, was hired each year from the capital by the ball committee, and the musicians knew well how Siddon Rock liked their Spring Ball dance programme, with waltzes and the Gay Gordons interspersed with the newer foxtrot and quickstep. At seven-thirty, there was a blast of sound from the hall as the band warmed up. This seemed to be the signal for pockmarks of light to move like will o' the wisps through the town, wavering towards the hall. As they came into Wickton Street the lights evolved into torches held low to illuminate the rough patches and potholes of the unsealed footpaths around the town.

Men in pressed dark suits and unfamiliar ties held the torches for women wrapped in coats or stoles against the chilly evening, as the women had both hands full holding their ball gowns high against the staining rub of gravel. *A mob of high-stepping possums, all fur and feet*, Bluey Redall remarked to Kelpie Crush as they leaned against the window counter, watching the parade down Wickton Street.

Why don't you go, Bluey? Kelpie asked as he shone up his cufflinks with a bar cloth.

Had enough of that sort of thing in London, Bluey said. *Can't be bothered now with all that dressing up stuff.*

What were you doing in London? Kelpie was vaguely interested.

Ah . . . bit of this, bit of that. Mainly what I know best. Bar work. I was born in this pub, ya know . . . was my dad's. I met Marge there, in London. Bluey was unusually forthcoming about his past. *In a jazz club, it was. Boy, could she play that clarinet, she was really something. Anyway, ancient history. Off you go, then. I can deal with the few that'll be in. I'll see you tomorrow.*

In the hall, about this time of the evening David Aberline usually tested the microphone and joked around with the waiting band. But this year Fatman would do the job, and was yet to arrive.

Among the cars making their way into the town was the old Ford belonging to Young George Aberline. The car had been bought anonymously at the clearance sale and left at the Two Mile for him.

Young George had said to Brigid Connor, as he helped empty bags of superphosphate into the spreader ready for the spring sowing, *My heart just isn't in it. Don't think we'll go at all.*

Don't want to tell you what to do, Brigid replied, *but it seems to me that this is just the year you SHOULD go. Don't let the bastards get you down.*

It's not that so much, Young George said. *But it just won't be the same without David there. He loves all that hoopla – the dressing up and sashaying around.*

Maybe Hettie needs it more than you do. Brigid banged an empty superphosphate bag considerably harder than needed to get the dregs out. *It's been pretty rough on her too. And it's not like she had anything to do with it, is it? She just gets pulled along by whatever you want to do – always has done, always will do. So stop feeling sorry for yourself and take her to the ball.*

So Young George and Hettie went to the ball. They were quiet and withdrawn from each other, both wishing

David was safely there with them instead of who-knows-where.

In the hall, greetings were formal. *Evening, Doctor Allen. Lovely night, Mrs Hinks, if a bit on the chilly side,* as if they had not seen each other shopping at the Co-op that morning, nor stopped for a chat at the post office when getting the mail. As people arrived, the hall gradually took on an air of festivity, if tempered a little by the absence of David Aberline – *Heard from young David yet, George? How's Hettie standing up to it all?*

Just fine, Young George said. *Everything's fine. David's heading to France, I think. Back soon, I'm sure.* But it all became too much to bear, and he bundled Hettie into the car and went back to the Two Mile before the first dance started.

Fatman Aberline arrived at eight o'clock sharp. He went straight to the stage and signalled for a roll of drums: *Gentlemen, take your partners for the first dance, the Pride of Erin.* The Spring Ball was underway.

Outside the hall, Alistair Meakins waited anxiously, watching for Catalin to come down the street from the hospital. As Matron Helith passed him on her way in, he asked diffidently if Catalin had said she was coming. *Oh yes*, Matron said, *she was getting ready quite early. I thought she'd be here by now.*

🦋

No-one can guess what Catalin did in the hours after she found that her mother had died. As the town people barn-danced their way around the dance floor, was Catalin in shocked and tearful mourning? Maybe she sat dry-eyed, looking at her life and her mother's. It is known that the flow of time fluctuates at moments of great change, so maybe the six hours compressed into a few seconds; or they could have extended to encompass a whole life. Did she go to wake her son, to tell him that his grandmother had died? Unlikely, but who can know.

What is known, though, is that Catalin Morningstar walked into the Spring Ball with a battered cello case, into the gap between the Gypsy Tap that had just finished and the last waltz waiting to begin. There are various versions of the details, with some commenting on the elegance of her dress and wondering where she got it. *Much too European for a designer from the capital*, they said. *And that beautiful material in the gown. How could a kitchen-hand afford it, on her wage?* Others, more concerned with the non-reflective surfaces, thought she looked upset or even distraught, and rightly so, considering her mother had just died, but this was with the benefit of hindsight. Most agreed that she definitely did not look as if she belonged in Siddon Rock. *Much too exotic*, Martha Hinks said. *That wild black hair*, said Gloria Aberline. *It looked like she'd never combed it in her life.*

There were others who thought differently. Marge Redall, if any comment was made to her later, always said, *Well, I thought she was just magnificent.* Sybil Barber, too, saw a woman of steel and tension. Granna, ensconced on a lounge chair at the supper room door, saw what she saw, but never did comment to anyone about it.

Kelpie Crush, leaning watchfully against the back wall, thought she looked like the tiny bright moth that was on the table in the Strangers' Room at the hotel, and he slipped quietly away.

In the hushing hall, Catalin placed a chair at the front of the stage. She opened the cello case, took out the instrument, and stood waiting until the room was quiet enough for her to speak.

This cello was my mother's and my mother's mother's, she said, *back further than I know.* She spun it around on its spike so that the paintings on the back could be seen. *The pictures on it are from places where it has been and people who have played it.*

My mother died tonight. I know because her picture is here – she touched the picture. *How this happens I do not know. It just does. Neither do I know where she was when she died. Our house in Budapest was destroyed; she wanted me to leave but she wouldn't go with me. This is my place, she said. I'll find somewhere here. Until tonight I knew she was alive somewhere, because our cello told me this.*

Catalin spun the cello again and took the bow from the case. *It is always played by the daughter when her mother dies – in celebration of her life, you see, in mourning. There have been no sons in my family for as long as memory, so I do not know about sons. I do not know if my Jos will play when I die. But that is a long time in the future. Tonight, for you, the people of my new place, I play my music of my mother in Hungary.*

Catalin stepped out of her shoes and sat on the chair, pulling back the full skirt of her dress so she could hold the cello between her knees, leaning forward and over it slightly with her cheek touching its neck. She raised the bow and drew it across the strings, and from the cello came a wailing cry the like of which had never before been heard in Siddon Rock. The note filled the hall, then flew out into the street. It soared over the rock and the salt lake towards the inland where it died in the ancient silence. At the war memorial, where Nell sat listening to the music of the ball, the dingoes recognised the sound and joined the lament.

Catalin touched other strings, finding the flattened notes of the minor F key, and her music became her mourning. Gradually the listeners heard other threads in the music. The sounds of a city were dominant with the clanging rhythms of trams and trains, the shuffle and bustle of people in the street, and even the tinkle of teaspoons against cups in a café.

Then the music darkened, changing to the whistle and thump-boom of bombs, the roar of a building falling, and the tramp of many marching feet. There was no *leitmotif* of Catalin in Berlin, nor of Jos being born. This was not their story, but that of Viktoria Morgenstern.

For Macha, on her nightly patrol around the town, the music breached her protective shell and she marched through a gap in the sound and into a dark place. There, a cacophony of death filled the space – the bullets that, in another place and another time, could have been the angry buzzing of bees or wasps; the dull crump-thump of mortar shells damaging the earth; the animal screams of wounded and dying humans. She deserted the guarding of her town and fled to her shelter in the Yackoo where she felt safe in the seeming innocence of the bush.

Marge Redall walked across the vast emptiness of the dance floor and onto the stage where she picked up the clarinet of the band-player. For a moment she hesitated, but her blue notes, sending off sparks like a striking match, sounded the key, and she stood next to Catalin and played the story of Siddon Rock, improvising around the formal, structured music of old Europe.

The cello hesitated, and then followed the clarinet's lead, and their separate sounds ravelled together until it was not possible to tell where the music of one ended and the other began. The dominant sound was of the town itself. The melancholy of Henry Aberline, camped under his jam-tree on the rock, was relieved by the laughter of the women who visited him. Sounds of trees being felled, the roar of tractors and harvesters and the cockadoodledoo of the train coming to the station gave another rhythm, as did the toc-toc of balls bouncing: footballs from the showground oval, tennis balls thudding on rolled anthill courts, the distinctive thwack of cricket balls on willow, softballs connecting with round bats in the school ground.

Individual themes joined the music. Granna shuddered when the dissonance of Bert Truro's thread disrupted the harmony; but Marge Redall's clarinet soothed the discord and the music soared on.

On played the women, and slowly and irrevocably they wove the town's stories into a fabric as delicate and strong as parachute silk, a fabric that billowed into Wickton Street as it grew too large for the confines of the hall. It hovered over the houses until it was caught by the breeze and drifted off towards the inland.

Granna, in her chair by the door, heard the missing things: the sudden disappearance of the bouncing theme that she thought was Jos's thread, and the lack of a story that could have been Kelpie Crush's.

Nell, from the war memorial shadows, saw the fabric of the town rise from the hall. She alone saw the ripped hole where her own story should have been.

What happened at the Railway and Traveller's Hotel that night can only be conjectured, but for the rest of her life Catalin would keep returning to the variations, worrying at them like a dog with a bone.

In the room off the upstairs verandah, maybe Jos Morningstar stirred when the first wailing note of his mother's cello flew out of the hall and into the streets. He could have become anxious when the keening music was joined by the howling of the dingoes. It could have been then that he took the torch his mother had given him (*You can switch it on and shine it around the room. Then you will see there is nothing to be frightened by*) and went onto the verandah where he could see down the street to the hall. Everything would have looked normal.

From the verandah it would have taken only a small resolution to go down the stairs – he did not dress first, his clothes were still on the end of the bed in the morning – with the weak ray of the torch shining on each tread, so that small pale feet stepped into a pool of yellow light – left foot down, right foot down, feet together – to the last step that brought him into the hallway near the Strangers' Room. Maybe he tried to open the door to this room, remembering it from the time Kelpie Crush had taken him in to see the moths.

Did he go out into the street then or did he waver, remembering what Catalin had told him on the way to the pub that afternoon? (*You go to bed and stay there asleep all night.*) Who knows what a six-year-old remembers at times of anxiety, and to hear the music of his mother in distress may well have wiped everything from his mind.

What if – and again, it is only supposition – what if the boy heard something he recognised in the billowing music floating from the hall, something that frightened him, making him run to escape it, sending him rushing towards the bush?

Or supposing he stood there, not knowing what to do, and there was a voice from the shadows in the hall of the pub, the voice of someone he recognised and trusted (*This is a safe place, good people. You know them. You'll be fine*) and that someone took the boy away. Who would know why. There are some things those left behind should not think on, lest the imagination take them places too dark to escape.

Maybe none of these things happened and his disappearance was something else entirely.

Whatever it was, the only facts known were that Josis Morningstar was not in his bed at the Railway and Traveller's Hotel on the morning after the Spring Ball, and that his clothes were there, in the room, as if he had left – or had been taken – in a hurry. For the rest of the story: it was, of course, what may have happened, in the hallway of the pub, or in the street, or outside in the bush. That is the legacy of the unknown: questions and more questions. That is all there ever is.

CHAPTER ELEVEN

AFTER THE BALL IS OVER

The large things that happen to a place are just made up of snippets and pieces. Like bushfires – people do what they have to do at the time, but when they get together at the pub, at supper after church or at the C.W.A. meetings, and tell their stories, it becomes a whole thing, and even then there's always bits that never get known.

THE HUSH OF THE EARLY MORNING after the Spring Ball could have been just the normal Sunday sound, which was quieter than during the mundane, workaday week. Or it could have been the sound of reticence returning to the citizens of Siddon Rock after the amazing events of the night before. Whatever the stories told about this day, there was often mention of the town mourning before even Catalin herself.

This much was well known, from what Catalin told the searchers and Inspector Bailey of the capital police:

Very early, Catalin, full of tears for her mother, walked to the pub to get Jos. She went up the outside stairs and along the first floor verandah to the open French doors into his room. When Jos was not there Catalin went to the kitchen, thinking he would be looking for breakfast, but the humming of the refrigerators seemed loud in the dim room where blinds were still drawn and the wood-stove unlit.

Then she hurried back to the hospital, following the track made by Macha's nightly patrol, thinking he may have woken and decided to go home this way. As she ran up the steps to their rooms she expected him to jump at her as he did each morning, clinging to her waist like a monkey. *Monkey-Jos*, she'd laugh. *Little monkee-Josee*. Jos was not there, and the dirty green and grey colours that always hung in the corners now filled the room.

Catalin ran back to the pub. She tried to hide the fear in her voice when she woke Marge and Bluey Redall, who went and found Kelpie Crush. The alarm went out when Bluey said that he had looked in on Jos about half-past eleven, and *yes, there he was, sleeping like the baby he is. Definitely there. I covered him up*. Marge said she had opened his door on her way upstairs after she arrived home from the ball. *I'm sure he was there, asleep under the blankets*. But she couldn't swear on the Bible that it was Jos in the bed, and not a distorted shadow thrown by the street light, or maybe just a rumpled bundle of blankets.

Bluey Redall telephoned Sinclair Johnson, who went next door and woke Doctor Allen. On their way to the pub they stopped at Abe Simmons'. *Harry just walked past*, Abe said, and they hurried to catch up to him. At the pub they found others who had heard, and a search party quickly formed and spread across the town. *We'll find the little devil in someone's backyard or playing at the football oval*, they said.

So the searchers worked their way through the town, each time explaining that *young Jos Morningstar, the Balt kid, has gone missing, and d'ya mind if I just take a look in the backyard and the shed?* They looked under every tank stand and every accessible under-house. They opened every door, including the back and front doors of shops, checking behind counters and shelving. They went backstage at the Shire Hall in case he had been out before Gawain Evans had locked up the night before. The rear of the *District Examiner & Journal* office looked promising for a moment with the back door swinging open, but it had only slipped its catch. The library was opened, in case he had found a way in. *He knows many English words now*, Catalin told the searchers. *He loves going to the library.*

Harry Best went to every family who had children at his school, mentally ticking an attendance roll as he went. At each home he saw which children were there and asked when they had last seen Jos. *Just stay home today*, he said as he left. *No use making it all harder than it is.*

The Catholic priest abandoned the service as the members of his congregation left en masse. The women took their families home with a silent thanksgiving that the missing was not one of theirs, and the men joined the search.

On the way to the Two Mile Brigid Connor stopped her truck at the cottage and called Young George out. *The Balt kid's gone missing*, she said. *You gonna go help?*

Maybe he was thinking of David, or maybe his natural kindness impelled him, but need reached Young George in the dark place he had inhabited since the sale of his farm. *Kids can't just go off*, he said. *We've gotta look after our kids.* And with that, Young George Aberline rejoined the community of Siddon Rock.

At the Methodist church people were taking their seats when Bluey Redall entered and overrode Siggy Butow's protests at the interruption. *A kid's more important than your words*, the publican snapped. And so the last of the men in the town joined the search for Jos Morningstar.

These were things that were known to be done. Later, when they tried to put together the complete story, they found that it was like patterns in a cheap kaleidoscope bought at the Annual Show: only some pieces could be seen at any one time, and even these kept rearranging themselves.

Granna thought she knew the whole story, but she was not certain and so did not ever say anything. Nell knew, but when she tried to tell them they couldn't understand.

Harry Best, Sinclair Johnson, Doctor Allen and Abe Simmons were following Macha's patrol track around the outskirts of the town. They were passing the silo when they saw Kelpie Crush standing there looking up the track up the rock.

Are you coming or going, mate? Abe Simmons called to him.

Kelpie turned. *Just going up to check Henry Aberline's cave*, he said. *Seems like a place where a kid would hide out.*

Hey, your nose is bleeding, Doctor Allen said. *Let me look.*

It's just fine. Kelpie Crush sounded angry. But Doctor Allen was already gently feeling the swollen nose.

How did you do this? he asked. *It must have been a powerful thump, it could be broken.*

Buggered if I know, Kelpie said, pulling away from the doctor. *I must have misjudged and walked into a piece of rock. I didn't see anything but it felt like I was walking into a wall. I'll just keep going now and come to see you later.*

Harry went to put his hand on Kelpie's arm, to hold him back, but recoiled from the glare in the man's blue eye. He moved back and Kelpie ran up the track, disappearing quickly around a bend. Harry hid how shaken he was until later when the men talked about the strangeness of the day. Then he admitted he had feared the barman at that moment, and felt that he didn't know him at all; that he was suddenly a stranger.

Catalin did not stop. She walked the town over and over, calling to Jos in several languages. In the dust at intersections of the streets she wrote messages for him in combinations and shapes of letters no-one else could understand. In Hungarian she wrote *Jossy, ne felj!*, and *Lauf in irgendein Haus; dort findest Du Freunde* was in the barking text of German.

Some of the townspeople were uneasy with these public messages they could not decipher, but said, *It's only for a short time, until he's found.* But when Catalin wrote in chalk on the side of the Farmers' Co-op, *Jos, Ich hab Dich lieb*, Harry Best suggested, *If he can read this, he'll surely be home. Why don't you wait at the pub with Marge.*

I want to go home first, Catalin said, *to check my cello. Just in case it tells me something.*

Cat . . . I wish there was something I could do. Your mother yesterday; now Jos running off.

He will be back. Soon. I just want to make sure.

So Harry Best walked with Catalin to the hospital. She opened the cello case, hesitating a moment before taking it out. But on the back there was no picture of Jos and the text still read as it had the night before:

Margit Catalin 1879 to 1930 . . . Viktoria Margit 1899 to 1948 . . . Catalin Viktoria . . . Josis Matthieu . . .

At the pub Marge Redall made breakfast for the search party while Catalin sat at the kitchen table with the cello case beside her.

I feel so bloody helpless, Cat, Marge said. *It's the not being able to do anything except wait that's so frustrating. But he WILL be found.*

It's my fault, Catalin said.

No, love, no. Don't think like that. If it's anyone's fault, it's mine. It's my pub, so my fault.

It's my fault, Catalin repeated. *My fault. I should not have left him.*

➤

The whispers started later that morning, like the small *tic* of a match against striker. *Funny that the Balt woman don't cry,* someone said. This could have been anyone at all, but was probably Mary Placer, known for sobbing loudly and easily.

Marge Redall had no time for whimpering in any shape or form. *Don't be bloody stupid*, she snapped. *Not everyone turns into a wet rag at the drop of a hat.*

But the fuse had been lit.

Maybe she did it herself, and hid the body somewhere. She was really late to get to the ball. Maybe all that stuff about her mother dying was a cover. Maybe she got someone else to do it. Maybe . . . There were some who were convinced, but there were others who thought otherwise.

He must have been taken, they said, *by someone travelling through the town at night.* This had some serious consideration, but was generally dismissed when Bluey said that no-one had gone into the bar that night, either familiar or stranger. There were, however, one or two who held to this theory.

An unthinkable thing was raised in a small group, in a whisper. *Could it be someone in the town? Someone we know who has taken away the boy?*

Wonder where Kelpie got to, someone said. But this thought was too dangerous, and quickly pushed away.

The general agreement was that Jos had woken early and wandered away to play. He was out there some-where, and so he would be found.

After the town had been scoured, the searchers gathered at the pub and there was no argument that the police had to be called in from the capital. Young George Aberline got on the phone. *A kid's gone missing*, he said, and this was enough. *Three hours*, was the reply, *we'll fly a tracker out with Inspector Bailey. But it'll be three hours before we can get there – about lunch-time. Where can we land?*

Have to be on the road north of the town, Young George said. *Look for the largest salt lake, it's not far from the rock at the edge of town. Tell your bloke not to use the lake surface. It looks firm but he'd end up drowning himself.*

Back in the bar men clustered in uneasy groups. *They'll be here in three hours*, Young George said to the bar in general. *I'm not waiting around. Anyone who wants to come with me, I'm going to the lake. Then I'll push out to Brigid Connor's two dams. Bloody water's a magnet to kids. And I'm going to try to find Macha Connor – if anyone's seen a wandering kid, it'll be her. Just a minute—*

Young George walked into the kitchen. *Mrs Morningstar . . . Catalin . . . does Macha Connor know Jos?*

Catalin shook her head. *No. She has not met Jos, he is always at school when Macha walks with me. This is early in the afternoon. I am always home when Jos gets home.*

Nell watched the line of searchers move around the lake, and knew she could help. Ahead of the party, in the drying salt at the lake margins, Nell drew a map, and the story of Jos.

First she drew the area, the shape of the place, with the lake, the Yackoo and other areas of bush, the unmistakable bulk of the rock. After that she marked in each house and shop in the town with the war memorial in the centre. Then she took a thin sharp stick and drew figures – the search party where it now walked; the dancers of the night before; and another figure, in the town, at the salt lake, and at the edge of the bush. She drew the story of that early morning, when her dingoes had worried her with their restlessness and she had thought it was because the sky was hidden by the fabric of the town as it spread upwards and outwards from the hall.

As the searchers came near she stood up and waited for them to notice the story, but Harry Best was the only one who saw her, the only one who stopped. Nell waved her arms over the story. *What is it, Nell?* Harry said.

I c'n help ya. Nell pointed to the drawing, but all Harry saw were dots and lines and squiggles. *I c'n help ya*, Nell repeated. Harry waited. Nell pointed at the drawing. Harry looked at Nell enquiringly. *That's interesting, Nell*, he said, *but I've got to keep going.* It was then Nell realised that, for all his whiteman education, the school teacher could not read story.

Later that morning Macha Connor saw the drawing and stopped to look at it. There she saw a map of the entire region laid out, but most of the figures of people, drawn in fine lines, had all but disappeared. One figure was much larger than the rest and drawn deeper into the earth, but in the oozing salty mud it was difficult to distinguish whether it was a man on hands and knees or a dog. Certainly there was a tail, but the face appeared human. Macha looked at this drawing for a long moment, touched it with her rifle and continued on her way.

The searching men saw no trace of Jos anywhere near the lake, nor at the sheds of the company that used to be Geo. Aberline & Son Minerals. There was no small body wedged in the gigantic machines abandoned by the Bush Bashers and now rusted into skeletons at the edge of the Yackoo.

The searchers walked the two miles to Brigid Connor's farm where the low level of water in the dams revealed only two dead sheep that had stuck in the mud and drowned.

While they were searching, the men watched out for Macha Connor but she was nowhere to be seen. They returned to the pub in frustrated silence, to meet Inspector Bailey and the tracker.

Here are the entries from Inspector Bailey's notebook, made before and during his talks with Catalin.

1. *The capital police were contacted by telephone at 9.30 am.*
2. *Inspector Bailey flew the Cessna C34 to Siddon Rock with tracker Jimmy James, arriving at 12.45 pm.*
3. *Interview with Mrs Morningstar began at 1 pm. She was calm, controlled and not showing any visible anxiety.*
4. *The child always visits the patients in the hospital, especially the boy, Ralphie, who is permanently hospitalised in an iron lung from polio.*

5. The child is a loner.

6. He wants to be a photographer.

7. He is not frightened of the bush.

8. The child does not talk to anyone but his mother. The mother would not say why.

9. Mrs Morningstar is a reffo. They arrived eighteen months ago she says, but cannot remember the name of the ship.

10. When asked where she came from, Mrs Morningstar said Budapest, Prague, Vienna, Berlin. This last is suspicious.

11. I asked how she got to Australia, and Mrs Morningstar said she came via Russia, Afghanistan, Pakistan, India, Madagascar. I seriously question this. As far as I know there are no shipping lines through these countries.

12. The identity of Mrs Morningstar should be seriously questioned, as she admits to changing her name from Morgenstern on arrival in the town.

13. The morals of Mrs Morningstar, or Morgenstern, must also be questioned as she admits to never having been married.

14. The child's name is not Joe Morgan, as given me by the officer taking the call. It's Josis Morgenstern, or Jos Morningstar, which are evidently the same.

15. All people in the town are accounted for except the barman Robert Crush. No-one has seen him since around mid-morning of the day after the child disappeared.

Nell heard that a tracker was coming from the capital, so she waited on the war memorial steps. When the tracker arrived, he sat on the pub verandah while Inspector Bailey talked inside with Catalin and the men. Nell walked up, diffidently stopping on the pavement close to where he sat. *I c'n help ya*, she said. The tracker looked straight ahead. She tried again, not looking at him, but down at the pavement. *I c'n help ya.* This time she understood that he was not going to hear her. She left the town and stayed in her hut, making sure the dingoes did not stray out of her sight.

᠍

In the bar a group of men gathered around Inspector Bailey. *We gotta start right away*, Young George was saying. *There's a lotta bush out there, and a lot that ain't really been into yet. Or the plains towards the inland – who knows how far he could have got, if he went that way. And wild dogs – dingoes. We all know what they c'n do to a sheep so God help any kid who gets taken by one of them. If we can't protect our kids, then what bloody use are we?*

But those who heard him knew that what he really said was, *If we can't protect our kids, then there ain't no future anywhere.*

᠍

When the search party was being organised Kelpie Crush was nowhere to be seen. Bluey knocked on the door of the Strangers' Room and looked in Kelpie's bedroom, but there was no trace of him. *Just go,* Marge said, *I'll send him on after you when he gets back.*

A bloody mongrel with a yellow streak, Bert Truro muttered. *Better off without 'im.* Bert always saw the bad side of anyone and remembered too well that Kelpie Crush had snapped at him on the night Bert tried to burn Nell's hut.

Catalin wanted to go with the search party, but Inspector Bailey refused. *It's no place for a woman,* he said. Catalin, carrying the cello case on her back, went to the highest point of the rock from where she watched the group walk along the edge of the road. In front was Jimmy James the tracker followed closely by Inspector Bailey. Behind them was a motley group of townsmen and farmers. Some way behind them came Alistair Meakins, who had stopped to put a notice on the door of the shop: THIS SHOP WILL RE-OPEN WHEN JOS MORNINGSTAR IS FOUND.

At first the group moved rapidly, then Jimmy James slowed as they left the gravel road and headed across the open ground towards the salt lake. He indicated that the group should stay back behind him. He walked around carefully, pointing out several places to Inspector Bailey, and even from a distance Catalin could see the frustration and annoyance, and she wondered what caused it. She could not see the many footprints and churned-up earth from the searchers that morning.

She did see, though, Inspector Bailey signal the group to stop and wait, and she watched the tracker walk alone to the edge of the perpetual pool, to the salt ponds of what had quite recently been Geo. Aberline & Son Minerals, then back to the perpetual pool, occasionally shaking his head at whatever he saw on the ground.

In the waiting group, Young George looked at his watch. *Wasting bloody time, aren't we*, he said to the men sitting on the ground. *Half-past two already, and we're still hanging around like a bunch of sheilas.*

Still walking alone, the tracker followed the shoreline of the salt lake towards Sybil Barber's house. As he approached, Sybil came out carrying a hat and small bag. She spoke with Jimmy James for a moment, then joined the waiting group.

When Catalin saw Sybil walking towards the search party she rushed down the rock and ran to catch up, the cello case bumping up and down on her back. Inspector Bailey frowned on seeing the women. *We dunno how long this'll take*, he said. *And we dunno what we'll find. Better you wait at home.*

Sybil just ignored him, and Catalin said, *There can be nothing worse than things I saw in the war. This is my son.*

Catalin and Sybil stayed a few yards behind the main group, and Sybil looked at the heavy cello on Catalin's back. *Do you want to leave that at my house?* she said. *It'd be real quick to drop it off.*

Catalin shook her head. *This will tell me how Jossy is, even if not where. I must keep it.*

And the women walked on.

It was close to four o'clock when the searchers started to move away from the salt lake towards the north.

Jimmy James went ahead again, leading the group across pale, salt-infected land. The tracker followed the signs that no-one else could see, moving steadily towards the farm that had been Young George Aberline's. Then he turned towards the Yackoo. *That'd be bloody right*, Fatman Aberline muttered as they skirted the rusting hulks of the Bush Bashers' abandoned machinery, *right into the bloody Yackoo.*

But as they approached the Yackoo, at the margin where the cleared land changed to virgin bush, the tracker stopped the group with an extended arm. At the edge of the scrub stood Nell with her dingoes close to her.

Bluey Redall said to Marge that night, *And that Nell looked really different. I thought it was the sun in my eyes at first – you know, getting on in the afternoon. She didn't say nothing, but that tracker just backed off like he'd been bit. And you know what he said? Men're not allowed.* He paused, and shook his head in amazement. *Bloody men are not bloody allowed. Now don't that just take the bleedin' cake.*

And when the copper went to go around him, it was like he was a friggin' sheep-dog, Young George said over that evening's meal at the Two Mile. *He weren't angry or aggressive. He just stopped every move that copper made.*

Bert Truro, of course, in his telling of it, protested that he would have gone on but was pulled back by the other blokes. What he would leave out was his shock at the sight of Nell standing there. Each time he thought of it he remembered the night he tried to burn her hut and how, as he fumbled with petrol and matches, she had appeared at the edge of the clearing. The dingoes, then, had not seemed like the slinking scavengers he knew they were, but wild animals held back by her voice. He couldn't bear to think about, let alone tell, of how he turned and ran like a frightened cur to the safety of his utility truck.

But no matter what protests the men in the search party voiced, no matter that they made threats ranging from dismissal to castration, Jimmy James walked away and the strength of his conviction took them with him.

$\blacktriangleright$

When Nell stopped Jimmy James leading the search party into the Yackoo she beckoned Catalin and Sybil forward, then turned to Alistair Meakins who stood apart from the angry group gathered around the tracker. She raised her hand slightly and Alistair was suddenly taller and slimmer; but as Allison made to step towards Nell, Alistair pulled her back. The moment between swirled with a shrilling of future voices of the town which were as sharp as the razor with which Alistair shaved Allison's legs.

Nell saw the hesitation and dropped her hand, and Alistair went with the men who followed Jimmy James.

$\blacktriangleright$

As the men turned away, the women walked into the bush, the dingoes slipping from shadow to shadow, melting into the place. *Jos's not here now*, Nell said, *been here, but gone now*. Skirting whippy mallee trees with their many trunks, and bushy wattle, the women stayed close behind Nell, Sybil helping Catalin through the scrub that caught at the cello case with long fingers. Nell repeated, *Was here, Cata, this mornin'. Not now.*

Quite suddenly the thick bush gave way to a large clearing, a park-like space with tall, straight trees stretching skyward where their canopies touched together. Long shreds of bark hung from the trunks of some, as if stripped by a giant hand, revealing pale new wood. The sunlight slanted obliquely to the floor, turning the flushed bronze of the new growth eucalyptus to a stained and fiery roof, picking out papery, fragile-looking pink and white flowers that grew in the dark leaf litter and dead bark. In the cathedral silence the snap of a breaking limb was sharper than a rifle shot. Birdsong did not soar and echo, but hung in spiralling threads from the topmost branches.

In this space was a three-sided shelter, with strong branches wired together and a roof woven from small tree-limbs in several layers, so that it was waterproof. *Macha made this, when she was a kid*, Nell said. She pointed to a bedroll that lay near the shelter. *That's hers. She sleeps here some nights. Jos here last night. Macha too.*

How do you know? Catalin said.

Nell took the women back to where the thick bush met the edge of the open space and spread her hands wide, indicating the earth. The sunlit afternoon became the darkest time between night and early morning. Nell pointed at the floor of the Yackoo, at the earth that appeared unsullied and pristine, and Macha burst into the clearing. She made a small fire in a well-used ring of stones, and sat with her back against the tree that was the prop for the shelter. Her rifle lay across her knees.

A tiny light flickered between the trees, so small it could have been a firefly. It moved unsteadily into the clearing, and the torchlight lit small feet cautiously feeling their way in unfamiliar territory. The feet stopped for a moment, then moved towards the fire.

Through a shifting haze that took all sound, Catalin tried to move to the tiny glow of torchlight, but Nell held her arm, *Stop.* They watched as Macha Connor ran to Jos, picked him up and wrapped him in a blanket. She put him down on her bedroll by the fire, placed the second blanket over him, and sat by him until the grey chill of dawn.

At first light they saw Macha pick up her rifle, check that Jos was still asleep, and walk away. Then the picture dissolved and the bedroll became just three blankets in a heap next to a ring of stones.

Catalin scrabbled in the bedding, searching for anything of Jos. As she lifted the canvas groundsheet a camera fell at her feet. She opened the battered leather case and saw the inscription inside the flap: *Meinem Sohn Hansi. Halte dein Leben fest, in Liebe, Mütterchen.* She started to read it aloud, *My son Hansi, hold your life still . . .* but found that her voice could not find the words; her tongue could not shape the language of the mother's love, and in her voicelessness she realised her fragility in the world. The old army-issue blankets were rough against her face as she inhaled deeply trying to find Jos in the tight warp and weft of the fabric. The dense wool was foreign against her tongue. She shook the blanket hard but only dust flew out and the smell was that of earth.

Macha go this mornin'. Jos stay here, Nell said. *Then he go.*

When? Catalin demanded. *When did he go? Where?*

He's here this morning, Nell repeated. *Then, he went.*

Nell showed them where Jos walked away from the enclosed space, through the bush towards the north. She stopped at the furthest edge, where the Yackoo ended and open plains began. *Came out here. Macha too, later. But after – a trick thing. I can't tell.* Nell could have added that what she saw there she didn't want to believe, and so could not tell it.

Nell turned back towards Siddon Rock, but Catalin was taking the cello case off her back. She knelt on the ground and held the instrument so that the sun caught the writing through the long shadows cast by the trees. The three women read the inscription:

Margit Catalin 1879 to 1930 . . . Viktoria Margit 1899 to 1948 . . .
Catalin Viktoria . . . Josis Matthieu . . .

Does that mean he's all right? That there's no dates? Sybil asked hesitantly, glancing at Nell who was looking off into the distance.

I do not know. I do not know, I do not know. Catalin's voice cracked and rose in panic, and she knelt in the dirt with her arms around the cello until Nell and Sybil lifted her and took her back to the town.

When Nell stopped the search party entering the Yackoo, Jimmy James walked away from the group with Inspector Bailey. *Gotta get rid of these blokes,* he said to him. *They messed up things too much. Gotta go on my own now.*

Do you want me with you? the Inspector asked.

Nah. Just me.

Young George Aberline was vocal in his anger at being dismissed. *Bloody boong telling us what to do,* he snarled. *Who the fuck does he think he is?*

He's a bloody good tracker, that's what he is, Inspector Bailey said shortly. *And we've gotta give him the room to do what he does best – find people. It's thanks to you lot stamping around all over the tracks that he's having trouble finding anything.*

The group of men turned back towards the town, but Young George stood watching the tracker walk slowly at the edge of the Yackoo, heading steadily north. He saw him stop, look back towards the town and the lake, then continue on his way until the curve of the bush hid him from sight. Then Young George reluctantly turned away.

Jimmy James stopped often, sometimes squatting to see closer. Once he crouched for some time, examining what he saw on the earth, then looked back in the direction of the town and the road leading from it. He looked around the place closely, but could not find what he sought, and continued north, never deviating from the margin separating cultivated ground and bush.

The light was failing when he reached the extreme north edge of the Yackoo. He stopped, reading the story written there. He walked carefully and looked intently at an area close to the trees, then he bent down and picked up a .303 rifle shell. Standing as tall as he could, he looked out across the open plains towards the interior. There in the distance was a figure on the ground. How far away was this? However far it was, Jimmy covered the distance in no time at all, slowing to a walk as he came close and saw that the figure was a large dingo. A strange animal this, with darker reddish fur and broader shoulders than the local breed. Not one of Nell's dogs then, which were pale-furred and sleek. Jimmy James bent down close to the animal's head and looked into its eyes, but all he could see was the colourless stare of a dead dog.

Whatever Jimmy James surmised from the signs written on the earth, this was what he reported to Inspector Bailey and the men of Siddon Rock who were waiting on the verandah of the Railway and Traveller's Hotel:

There's dingo tracks everywhere, he said. *Boy and man tracks underneath. I can't read the ground right, it's all churned up. That swimming place, perpetual pool, in the lake – there could be boy tracks, but there's so many other*

*footprints over 'em, it's hard to say if they're going into the
lake or walking along the edge.*

*Out at the north end of the Yackoo I thought there
could be something. Looked like a man on the ground, but
it turned out to be a dead dog – maybe dingo, maybe dingo-
kelpie from the colour and size.*

Bert Truro sniggered into his beer. *Bloody old boong
gin'll be ropeable, havin' one of her mongrels killed.*

Jimmy James gave him an opaque look. *Not one of
Nell's,* he said. *Somethin' different than from around here. A
stranger.*

If anyone had asked Macha Connor about that day, and if
Macha could have answered, this is what she would have
told them.

Jos's entry into the Yackoo was lit only by the tiny,
wavering light of his torch. Such a small child, even for
his six years. Maybe Macha thought that he too had fled
from the music in the town that opened dark places
for her. But the frightened child was no threat and she
picked him up. She put him in her bedroll near the fire
and watched over him.

Macha moved when the sun slipped obliquely
through the trees. She left Jos sleeping by the hut and
walked towards the town, taking the short route over the
rock. At the peak, she stopped and looked down into the
streets where groups of people moved from house to house,
and men clustered on the pub verandah. Puffs of dust

rising from the roads leading out of town marked where cars had recently driven away, and there were none of the usual Sunday sounds of music and singing from the various churches. The activity was too much for Macha, and she turned around, heading for the Two Mile, where she collected food and water. When she returned Jos had gone, but Macha easily followed his tracks through the bush to the north edge, until they disappeared on the hard ground.

By now the sun was directly overhead and threw no shadows. Macha looked out to the horizon where the margin between open plains and sky blended into a shimmering water-like mirage. As she searched the distance, eyes squinted against the glare, a figure appeared in the vertiginous light. To see more clearly, Macha lifted her rifle and looked along the sights, but the figure was still amorphous; at one moment it appeared to be a man, at the next it could have been a large dog or a dingo. What she was certain of was that it carried a bundle that looked like a child. The figure was not moving towards Siddon Rock but towards the inland.

There are points in a life when all that was and all that could be condense into a single moment and force a decision. Some have the moment at a turning point, a cusp of events that unexpectedly wedges itself into daily happenings. This is how it was for Catalin who, when she realised she was pregnant, knew she would leave the chaos of war-infested Germany.

For Macha Connor, who had been shown how to see by her mother's farmhand lover Mellor Mackintosh – *Ya gotta trust what ya see* – that moment was when she saw a bundle that could have been a child being carried away. She tucked the butt of the rifle firmly against her shoulder, but the sights were clouded by the ghosts. They crowded around, and a sly, sibilant mutter started as they pushed the gun barrel down. Macha hesitated, then she re-focused, held the weapon firmly and gently squeezed the trigger, shooting through the throng who had travelled home with her from the war. Then she ran, flying across the hard ground, expecting to find a dead man and a child. But there was no child, just a dying dog who looked at her with a hate-filled blue eye.

At dusk that same day Jimmy James would try to read the story Macha left embedded in the earth at the edge of the Yackoo. He too looked out and saw a man or a dog, but he could see no tracks on the hard earth to lead him to where it might have taken Jos Morningstar.

When Kelpie Crush had not returned by the following morning, Bluey Redall opened the Strangers' Room for Inspector Bailey. Inside was the paraphernalia of a collector. On the table were grubs and insects in jars and several sheets of paper were partly covered by pinned moths. Obviously cut from newspapers and magazines, pictures of insects of all kinds littered the table and were stuck to the walls, along with recipes and pictures of unrecognisable food.

Bit of a mess, the policeman said, *but nothing's here.*

After the bar closed for the night. Bluey Redall said to Marge, whose blue notes were particularly dark and silent at that moment, that the Strangers' Room was *a real dog's breakfast. And that copper, he didn't reckon it was strange, even though he looked at it. Just you come and have a look.*

Bluey opened the door to the Strangers' Room, which swung wide against the inside wall. *Looks fine, even if it is a bloody mess*, Marge said. Then Bluey closed the door, shutting them in. *Now look.* Stuck to the door was a patchwork of tiny black and white photographs, each one of a boy.

They look like the proofs of school photos from last year, Marge said. *Why on earth would he want them?*

Yeah, Bluey said, *but not all the kids are there, just the boys in the cub scouts. And look how there's a moth pinned through some. Those night-flying ones that bump around the lights. Why some and not others?*

But didn't Jos join a while back? And there's not a photo of him, Marge said. *I wonder why?* She looked at each tiny photo carefully. *Here's Will Hinks. And Barry Aberline – from that lot down past the south road turn-off. We know all these kids, Bluey.*

But there's not one of Jos, Bluey repeated. *Look here.* He pointed to a white space at the centre of the picture display that had only a large brown moth pinned to it. *There's been a photo here, and it was taken down. You can see the pin-marks where the corners were. No photo, just the bloody moth. Why?*

Buggered if I know, Marge said. *But I think I know where you're going with this, and I don't want to think about it. If the cops say there's nothing in it, let's just leave it at that, eh.*

I suppose we can't do anything about anything, anyway. Bluey started picking up paper from the floor. *We'd better clean this mess up.*

Marge peered down the microscope that had a moth under its viewer. *Just look at this. They look so fragile, the wings. And there's such a pattern on them. Like a piece of tapestry. There's blue and green and brown – so many different shades. You'd never think it, looking at it normally. And what's the difference between a moth and a butterfly, anyway?*

Beats me, Bluey said as he threw jars and cookbooks into a box.

Maybe it's that butterflies come out during the day and moths are around at night, Marge said. *Guess there's always a dark side of everything, eh. Like light and dark of the same thing. Can you finish up here? I've got to clean up in the kitchen.* She walked off, then hesitated and came back to Bluey. *Do you think I'll ever not feel guilty, Blue*, she said, *or will it be here for the rest of my life?*

Bluey put his arms around her, awkward at the intensity of the moment. *Nothin' for you to be guilty for, love. It's me who's at fault. I was supposed to be lookin' after him. Guess I'll just have to wear it.*

Guess we'll both just have to wear it, Marge said. *Both of us.*

That Kelpie Crush disappeared the same day as Jos Morningstar was the talk of the town for weeks. Some worried at it, trying to find meaning, but most people agreed with the comments of Brigid Connor. *He was a stranger*, she said, *and we knew nothing about him. He could've taken young Jos, or not, we'll never know. But there's nothing we can do about it all.*

Here are some pieces of the town's recollections of Robert (Kelpie) Crush. That he seemed to be terrific with the kids in the cub pack, which fell apart after he disappeared. That he was too good to be true, all that smarminess to everyone. That Abe Simmons never did like him, although he never actually caught him cheating at poker. That Harry Best had been to talk with him, when he first came to town, about his worthiness to start a cub pack, and told everyone he was suitable. There were one or two – no names being said – who thought Harry should be held responsible, but most said that was going too far. Those who leaned on the bar of the pub knew he pulled a good beer and never said anything about anyone. Marge and Bluey Redall were probably the only ones who suspected that he never slept. And Sinclair Johnson was heard to declare quite often, *That bloke saw and heard more than we knew*, until told by Sybil Barber to *put a plug in it and move on to something else.*

It was also remembered that Harry Best, Sinclair Johnson, Abe Simmons and Doctor Allen were the last ones to see Kelpie Crush as he dashed up the track over the rock.

At the Tuesday night poker game, the week after the disappearances, the talk was of their last sighting of the man. Sinclair Johnson and Abe Simmons couldn't agree on whether he had been going up the rock, as he told them, or was coming back from somewhere. Could have been either, Harry Best said, reminding them that Kelpie had been standing still when they first saw him. *Looked to me like he could have been coming or going. But remember his nose?*

Yeah, Doctor Allen said – he'd been roped in to make a foursome – *It was broken, I reckon. Looked like he walked into something really hard. However he did it, it had taken a real thump.*

Harry poured himself another scotch and added a splash of water. *He said he walked into something that felt like a wall*, he said. *Maybe the rock knows something we don't about what happened, and was trying to stop him from getting away. There's more things in heaven and earth . . .*

Bloody hell, Sinclair Johnson interrupted, *if that's the sort of nonsense you teach the kids! Bloody rocks knowing things! You're losing it, mate. No more scotch for you! Rock is just rock. Nothing special. No life. Just bloody hard dirt.*

For the rest of his life, Harry Best brought out the memory in the dark of the night when he couldn't sleep, and wondered if he could have stopped it all at the beginning when he talked to Kelpie Crush about starting a cub scouts pack in the town and decided he had no need to check further on the charming stranger.

But apart from snippets and fractured memories passed from those who were there to their children, there is little in the town to remind of Robert Crush, known as Kelpie, who was the barman at the Railway and Traveller's Hotel during and after the war.

Marge Redall packed up the collection of moths and insects, and took it to Gawain Evans at the Council Offices where she said, *I reckon these should be kept, but not at the pub.* Gawain put the boxes in an unused cupboard in the boardroom where they were promptly forgotten, except maybe by Granna.

Macha, on her way to patrol the town, stopped at Nell's hut. Nell touched her on the arm. *Not one of mine*, she said.

At least we know where David is, Young George said to Hettie as she prepared the evening meal. *At least we know.*

Mach might have come home not speaking, Brigid said to Granna. *But at least she's home.*

To the town, Catalin appeared calm and controlled, so much so that the whispers that had started the day Jos disappeared became louder and more overt; sibilant, like bees swarming around something sweet and irresistible. When she walked down Wickton Street the women would give a small half-smile that carried the shape of thin-lipped disapproval, and glance away. The men still doffed their hats, but the desire lurking at the back of their eyes became less obvious, and thoughts of their uncomplicated wives rose unbidden to mind.

Every night Catalin sat in the room where Jos had slept. She could not sleep, but refused to take Matron's offer of time off. *Where would I go?* she said. *At least here I can do something.* But she floated around the hospital like a ghost, so that Matron hired Martha Hinks' daughter to help out for a while.

I've never heard her cry, Matron said to Nell. *It's not healthy to bottle it all up inside. It's like an abscess, the bad has to come out to be healed.*

CHAPTER TWELVE

GOOD SALT

To cleanse the soul you must wash in someone's tears.

Viktoria Margit Morgenstern 1899–1948

EARLY MORNING ON THE ROCK is as profound as the grave, as if time itself is suspended. The grey time before dawn holds remnants of the night and the first signs of the coming light.

There she is, Catalin, as high as she can get on the rock. Not as high as the flight of cockatoos that rises up from the station-yard, spiralling over the town towards the light. Not nearly as high as she would like to be, flying over the inland until she finds Jos and brings him home. All she can do is sit here watching so that she will see him immediately he appears. There have been no tears. There is no reason for tears. *Save your tears for things that need them*, her mother had always told her. *There are always those worse off than yourself.* So Catalin cannot cry for something that will soon be righted when Jos comes home.

There, too, is Macha Connor. She has finished her patrol around the town and is but a few steps away from where Catalin sits. This is the morning ritual now: the patrol, the climb, and sitting here with Catalin until she has to start at the hospital.

This morning there are others on the rock. On the west side Nell is climbing easily, the dingoes running ahead and behind, shepherding her up the steep slope. She arrives a moment or two after Macha, at the same time as Sybil Barber.

Nell knows what she must say to Catalin. *Gotta do something*, she had said to Sybil the day before. *Gotta make her see that the kid's gone; not comin' back. All that salt she's hangin' on to gotta come out before it makes her die inside.* But to herself she said, *Can't tell her it all. No need to tell it all.*

The women sit with Catalin, gazing out across the bush of the Yackoo. *Look at the railway track,* Catalin says. *I wonder where it ends. I wonder if Jos will be able to get a train back.*

Sybil, too, looks to the inland. *Ends up at a siding about fifty miles out*, she says. *You know, when I was a kid I'd sit up here every Christmas morning. There was this song, see, that we'd sing at school.* And she sings:

I saw three ships come sailing in,
on Christmas day, on Christmas day,
I saw three ships come sailing in,
on Christmas day in the morning.

And I'd come here and wait for the three ships to come in across the salt lake – which wasn't nearly as big as it is now, but seemed pretty huge to a kid.

Well, one year – I was seven or eight – I was here real early, like now. It was light, but before the sun came up. Alf had belted Mum during the night, knocked her out so that she wouldn't know what he did to me, I think. He used to treat me like . . . like his wife. So I climbed out the window and came up here. There I was, feeling pretty miserable and hating the world. Then a train went flying past, just a rattly old wheat-truck thing. It missed the branch-line to the silo, and it stopped suddenly, all shaking and noise, and backed up. But as it did I could hear the driver and the stoker laughing, and they started pulling the whistle. Cockadoodledoo, it went. Cockadoodledoo, as if there was something to be happy about.

Then the sun started to come up, and I'd never seen anything like it, probably because I'd not got up that early before. Just a pink smudge it was, sitting on the edge of the inland for ages. All of a sudden it rushed up, as if it was pulled by a string, this huge reddy-gold ball. Straight up into the sky, and for a few minutes the salt was pink. There was a gorgeous sparkly pink salt lake and the plains were bright red. Sybil swept her arm in an arc, indicating the vastness of the country at their feet.

But the thing is, way out there at the edge of the world I could see three shapes sailing out of the pink haze. All shimmery they were, and kept changing shape. But I knew they were three ships come sailing in. I could see the sails, and how they rocked up and down the waves. And when I squinted my eyes against the sun, I could see people on the decks, all dressed in caftans and turbans, just like the pictures in the books at school. And I knew, I just knew, that these were my ships, coming to take me away from here. I don't know how you did it, Catalin. Coming to a place like this, from Europe. It must have been hell.

No, Catalin says, *there was hell. Here is limbo. This is worse.*

Nell signals the dingoes to stay away, and walks up to Catalin. *You trust me, eh, Cat? You know that I'd not tell you wrong?*

Catalin nods.

Gotta say this, Cat. I gotta say this. You listen and gotta believe me. He's not coming back, you know.

How can you know that? Catalin picks up a stone and hurls it out. It twists in the air and flecks of fool's gold flash in the first rays of the sun. *How can you know?*

Remember the Yackoo, Sybil says. *Nell knows.*

I know, Nell says. *I read it on the land.* She glances at Macha. *And that Kelpie Crush. Well, he's not comin' back either. Macha fixed him.*

Catalin stands there on the topmost point of the rock, and the sound she makes is not a scream, not a cry, but rather a howl of primal emotion for the lost child.

Nell gathers Catalin to her, rocking and crooning until the sound becomes tears. *We don't know, Cat, why he left the pub, eh. Never know. You gotta let it go, just a little bit. Not try to know things we can't know.*

Sybil walks away a few steps, her face tight as she stops her own tears.

It's good to cry, Nell murmurs to Catalin. *Bad salt inside, good salt out, eh. You cry, Cat.*

I'm so tired, Catalin says. *Bone-weary.* She leans against Nell. *It's my fault, for coming here. My fault for leaving him alone. I promised he'd be safe there.*

Macha takes Catalin's hands, looking intently into her face. She shakes her head and taps herself on the chest. *Not your fault*, says the gesture. *My fault.*

No, Catalin says. *No. You try to guard the town – everyone in the town. You can't watch everyone, Mach. Not all the time.*

I told Jossie I would always come to get him, so I must always be here. Just in case. But I will never stop crying, here inside. Never.

CHAPTER THIRTEEN

Nell, do you know the other name for this rock?

Yeah, Jack told me.

Can you tell me?

Yad Yaddin.

What's it mean?

In your lingo, means 'stay here'.

ACKNOWLEDGEMENTS AND THANKS

It is not possible to list all those who contributed to this book in so many different ways. You know who you are, and I extend my heartfelt thanks. I have found that those with the knowledge are always generous with it, and I accepted all offerings gratefully. There are some who went way beyond the line of duty or friendship, when asked, and the following thankyous are in no specific order, for everything added to the whole in different ways:

Nigel Krauth, for his endless patience and generosity of knowledge; Dr Tess Meyer (Germany) and Christine Balint for help with the German and Hungarian languages; Roland Breckwold for his advice on dingo behaviour; Marianne Horak of the CSIRO, who taught me about naming insects and who named the butterfly; the several professional readers who made wise suggestions, particularly Judith Lukin-Amundsen and Geoff Hancock (Canada); and to Beverley Edwards who gave me open access to her home whenever I needed a quiet space to work.

I received financial support from artsACT that allowed me to spend time at Varuna, where much of the first draft was laid down. There are moments in the stories that evolved from the old children's encyclopaedia I found in the cottage where Eleanor Dark used to work. The professionalism of Lyn Tranter of Australian Literary Management and Meredith Curnow and Elizabeth Cowell at Random House brought this book to fruition.

QUOTED SOURCES

21–22 'Hush Little Baby' – traditional lullaby

35–36 Sonnet CXXIV – William Shakespeare

70 'Dance with a Dolly (with a Hole in Her Stockin')' – words and music by Terry Shand, Jimmy Eaton and Mickey Leader (copyright © 1940, 1944 Shapiro, Bernstein & Co., Inc., New York; copyright renewed; international copyright secured; all rights reserved; used by permission)

90 Genesis 3:19, King James Bible

127 'Comin' thru the Rye' – traditional Scottish song, based on a poem by Robert Burns

141–142 'Talking in Their Sleep', Edith M. Thomas, 1908

170 '*Once when it was not, beyond seven times seven countries . . .*' – traditional opening words of Celtic storytellers, used to open a path to the Otherworld for the listener

179 'Rock of Ages' – Augustus M. Toplady, 1776

180 Sirach 13:15-17, King James Bible

181 Deuteronomy 33:17, New Standard Revised Version

184–185 'Chickery Chick' – words by Sylvia Dee, music by Sidney Lippman, 1945 (reproduced with permission of Albert Music)

198 'We Plough the Fields', Matthias Claudius, 1782

199–200 'Bringing in the Sheaves', Knowles Shaw, 1874

201 Revelations 14:11, King James Bible

278 'I Saw Three Ships Come Sailing In' – traditional carol

AUTHOR'S NOTES

The town of Siddon Rock is a wholly fictional creation, and not to be confused or conflated with any town in existence. I was influenced strongly by three other fictions that wrote about place: Kim Scott's *Benang* (Fremantle Arts Centre Press, 1999), which maps the Aboriginal story in the south-west of Australia; Robert Kroetsch's *What the Crow Said* (Edmonton, University of Alberta Press, 1988), the story of the fictitious town of Big Indian, Canada; and Jack Hodgins's *The Invention of the World* (Toronto, Macmillan, 1977), set on Vancouver Island, Canada.

Similarly, all characters in this novel are fictional and not representative of any person either living or dead.

The name Yad Yaddin for the rock comes from my own family history, which has it that it means 'stay here'. Whether this is factually so, or not, for this piece of fiction this is what it means.